Beyond Life
(The Afterlife Series Book 2)
By Deb McEwan

Cover Design by Jessica Bell

The Story So Far

Thanks for choosing 'Beyond Life', book two in my Afterlife Series. If you haven't read the first book ('Beyond Death',) I recommend you read it before this one. Here's a reminder of the story so far.

I recommend you read them before this one. Here's a reminder of the story so far.

Big Ed has coerced three teenage girls into accompanying him to a party with the offer of free food and booze. They're unaware they will be groomed to have sex with older men. Melanie smells a rat, changes her mind and leaves the car before it reaches its destination.

Claire Sylvester dies in a RTA the morning after the best night of her life, along with Ron, her taxi driver. Her twin brothers Tony and Jim know she's dead before being told.

An angel named Gabriella tell Claire and Ron there's a backlog of souls waiting to be processed due to a natural disaster on earth. They're kept at Cherussola until the Committee decide their future, but are allowed to visit their friends and family. Claire discovers that her fiancée had a one-night stand with her best friend, and that her parents' marriage is a sham. Her father has been living a double-life for many years and she has a half-sister called Melanie. She also discovers she can communicate with her brothers and that she has powers that many dead souls do not.

Ron discovers his wife had an affair with Ken, his former boss. Ken dies and goes to Hell. He is reincarnated in different forms and his soul is in constant fear and pain.

Claire's mother Marion and Ron's wife Val meet by chance and join a charity. At a get together Tony meets Val's daughter Libby; they become romantically involved.

Val is already in a delicate state due to her husband's death. She is mugged (by three humans and one evil soul) during a training course and Ron begs Claire to do everything in her power to bring the muggers to justice. They discover where the muggers live and hang out, then hatch a clever plan to catch the muggers, involving Claire's twin brothers and Jim's girlfriend Fiona.

Melanie's friends tell her about their ordeal so she informs the police. She is kidnapped by Big Ed and his accomplice Sandy. Claire helps her brothers to find and save Melanie, but Big Ed escapes along with Sandy. He loses his temper and kills Sandy.

Having observed Claire and Ron's work with the twins, the Committee inform Gabriella that Claire is to remain where she is for a while to help people, while the angels are busy dealing with the backlog. Ron has the choice of whether to remain with Claire, or to move on to eternity. Claire is sent back to Earth to visit her family and friends, not knowing whether Ron will be in Cherussola when she returns.

Chapter 1

According to the Committee it had taken centuries to break him but finally it had happened. His optimism about the goodness of people failed him, and he focused on the less than one per cent of the human race who were intrinsically evil. They said that God had had a nervous breakdown and was no longer in charge of the Committee.

*****

Gabriella was busy supervising a number of grade five spirits in their mission to bring Sandy to Cherussola when she received a call to put Sandy's journey on hold. She was told to appear in front of the Committee as a matter of urgency. Had she been a lower grade she would not have had the courtesy of a call. The juniors looked at her, none of them realising the seriousness of the situation. Their faces were masks of confusion and their indecisiveness showed a complete lack of leadership amongst one and all. It wasn't the first time that Gabriella silently wished for the company of the feisty Claire and her more sensible, but less talented companion Ron.

'Alex, Colin, you two are in charge. Keep her here until I return and concentrate, I don't want the evils to get hold of her,' she resisted the urge to say *yet* and disappeared in a whoosh before the usual torrent of questions. This new batch she'd been given to train-up were distinctly below average and would try the patience of a saint.

Standing in front of the Committee Gabriella's intuition had served her well and she had correctly assumed that they'd changed their mind about Sandy's fate.

'But look what that poor woman's been through. Surely she deserves a chance at redemption?'

Raphael looked at his twin sister and nodded. He remained seated at the table when he spoke.

'I agree with Gabriella. She's suffered throughout her adult life and doesn't deserve to go to hell,' he looked at the eleven in turn before his eyes rested on his mother. 'Surely we should give her a chance at the very least?'

Amanda studied her son and daughter. She'd promoted Raphael to the Committee hoping that Gabriella would be jealous and their bond would lessen, but to no avail. If anything it had made them even closer. And when she needed Raphael to support her, he sided with his sister apparently not overly concerned with the consequences. Well, he should be.

She stood up and pushed her chair away from the round table. Its shape implied a democracy but Amanda had taken charge a number of years ago due to the indecisiveness of the other Committee members. She looked around now and her smile rested on God. She remembered what he'd been like before the never-ending round of war, famine and murder had finally taken its toll and caused his nervous breakdown, and a major loss of confidence. Nevertheless his counsel was wise and generally accurate and he was happy as long as he didn't have to make the final decisions. She'd discussed Sandy's case with him privately before the meeting and decided that the woman should be punished for her weakness in adult life.

'Remember the parties where the evil man sold young girls to his sick clients?' they murmured in agreement.

'Well Sandy often drugged the drinks of those young girls and...'

'But she also saved the one that was kidnapped,' Gabriella interrupted, exasperated at the way the meeting was going.

'I agree.' Raphael sided with his sister yet again.

Amanda gave her children a look that silenced them. 'We all know how much those girls suffered. Some have been able to put it behind them, some are still suffering and all are scarred for life. Now we vote.'

Discussion over, Amanda asked for a show of hands for those in favour of sending Sandy to hell and damnation. All but Raphael voted with her.

'Decision made. Now to other business.'

All heads turned to Raphael at the sound of his chair scraping along the floor.

'I can't do this any more,' he was trying his best to stay calm but his fists were clenching with the effort as he stood up. Gabriella knew the signs and so did their mother. His sister walked toward him and placed a hand on his upper arm for both support and restraint.

'It was a mistake and you were promoted too soon. You still have a lot to learn, son.' Amanda was determined that her son's demotion would be her decision and not his. 'Rejoin your sister's team and try not to get too emotionally involved.' She turned away from him dismissively, hiding her disappointment well. Gabriella pulled her brother's arm none too gently, willing him to keep quiet as they left the Committee Chambers.

He vented his anger once they were out of earshot. 'I don't believe it. It seems so wrong,' he banged his fists together in frustration. 'There are many worse than her who've made it and proved their worth, and some who haven't.'

Gabriella listened as he let off steam and listed an extraordinary amount of names and dates. Some of them she'd forgotten and as usual, her brother's memory and attention to detail never failed to amaze her.

He stopped suddenly, deflated.

'Look what you've given up, Raphael for a point of principle. I hope it was worth it?'

'Truth be told the novelty wore off and though I hate to admit it, Mum was right,' he winked at his sister, his calm demeanour returning as quickly as it had left him. 'I'd much rather be where the action is.'

She knew he was trying to make good of a bad situation and although jealous when he'd been the most junior angel promoted to the Committee, she was also very proud of him and sad that he'd been removed. It was a double-edged sword though, despite the initial disappointment Gabriella did need help on her team and was grateful to have someone she could trust one hundred per cent.

*****

Sandy's journey upwards in a sea of warm loving hands made her smile with wonder and awe at her first impressions of death. No longer would she have to tolerate the abuse from Big Ed and be complicit in his acts of evil. She had no idea what was going to happen next but the hands touching her seemed to radiate goodness and she relaxed and allowed herself to enjoy the experience. She felt a rough jolt and dropping sensation, as if on an aircraft that had suddenly lost height, and the pleasantness disappeared in the blink of an eye. The soft gentle hands were no more and fingers poked and prodded. She looked down in horror. Some were bloody, some without nails, others half-eaten by maggots. The fear that she'd experienced while alive on Earth magnified ten-fold. Sandy squeezed her eyes closed and screamed but nobody came to help. Still screaming she was taken through the dark gates to receive unfitting retribution for allowing herself to be too weak-willed and easily led in her last life.

The pain in her earthly life had been easy in comparison to what Sandy was forced to endure next, and she lost all track of time. The agony of her skin on fire, boiling blood being dropped into her eyes and thousands of insects crawling into every orifice and eating her from the inside out couldn't be properly defined, and Sandy regretted every weakness and bad decision she'd made on Earth.

Whenever she thought the pain and humiliation was over for a while, something else happened and she felt like a hamster on a wheel spinning with pain. This time she appeared in the dark circle. All was quiet until she heard someone retching. The sound was soon accompanied by another then another and before long that was all she could hear. The first lot of vomit hit her on her chest and she watched as the fluid dribbled downwards except for one stray carrot piece that remained stuck between her breasts. From her previous experience she knew that worse was to come and it wasn't long before all the demons were puking on her. She looked around at the sea of sick and realised what her fate was to be on this occasion. Screaming and crying did her no good but that didn't stop her, and she screamed until she gagged on the viscous liquid and could scream no more.

Despite or maybe because of the pain and indignity Sandy refused to cooperate with the demons. She knew they were lying when they told her the pain would stop if she would follow their orders and carry out their heinous crimes against the living, and those dead like her. She was determined not to sell her soul to the devil and her experience with evil people while living meant that she easily recognised the lies she was being fed. So, she endured and when she next opened her eyes experienced her first life in the body of an animal. It took a moment for Sandy to realise that she was being humped. When she struggled, the teeth dug

deeper into her back so she remained still and suffered
in silence. When he'd finished, the rabbit jumped off
and Sandy moved away from him as quickly as she
could. Realising she was hungry, she sniffed her way
towards some fresh grass. Before she arrived at the spot
she was looking for Sandy was being jumped again. It
was not enjoyable and she looked around while the
animal on her back had his way with her. The scene
was being replicated throughout the field and the look
on the faces of the other female rabbits mirrored that of
Sandy's. The males seemed to be aggressive and overly
cruel and she wondered if these were genuine animals
or, like her, had been sent here to suffer or to make
others suffer. They certainly weren't the fluffy type
she'd encountered during her time as a human. After
the fourth time she could take no more and made a bid
for escape. Running for all she was worth, Sandy was
being pursued by at least four randy bucks. There may
have been more but she daren't slow down to count
them. Her heart was beating too fast and she was
exhausted but still she ran. Eventually the strength of
her followers prevailed and she was caught. They took
it in turns, time and time again and finally her torn and
exhausted body could take no more. Her days as a
rabbit were over but there was no relief for her as she
was returned to the pits of hell.

It was the flapping that brought her round this
time. Sandy assumed it was birds but then remembered
that she had liked birds when living and knew she
couldn't be that lucky. As she slowly opened an eye she
couldn't take in what she was seeing first of all. Her
whole body seemed to be moving but she was
completely still. Then a moth the size of an eagle
hovered right in front of her face. Sandy closed her eyes
and took a deep breath. She started sweating, trying to
tell herself that her moth phobia was irrational and that
they couldn't hurt her. But these were no ordinary

moths. The pain of the flesh being ripped from her body was excruciating and she called for help and salvation, but when the demons came, she still refused to agree to be their slave.

Sandy's endurance, regret for her weakness in life, and refusal to join the evils frustrated the demons. They could only claim those that were pure evil or who would turn to pure evil and Sandy's soul was neither. Gabriella's spies had informed her of Sandy's actions and Gabriella had listed them for the Committee's attention. Gabriella and Raphael had discussed their options and decided their best chance was to approach their mother, rather than copy the details to all members of the Committee. Amanda didn't call a meeting this time but brought Sandy's actions to the attention of the Committee by way of a memo. It wasn't unusual for the occasional soul to be saved from Hell and given a second chance, so Amanda didn't see any need to admit that a mistake had been made. They all agreed that Sandy had showed bravery and fortitude against all odds and her soul deserved another chance. So it was towards the end of her next animal incarnation that she was to be brought to Cherussola.

Being a dung beetle wasn't so bad Sandy considered, trying to convince herself as she softened the manure before chewing on it. She certainly preferred this life to that of a female rabbit, which had involved more pain and fear. Whatever happened, it always ended in pain and fear, and the laughter of the angry demons who actually seemed to enjoy her agony and the journey back down there. Then it all started over again. Yes, eating shit was definitely preferable to that. She was a dung beetle and should enjoy it but no matter how hard she tried, it still tasted like shit and she gagged every time she tried to swallow. She knew that not eating would make her weak and lessen her chances of survival but Sandy couldn't help herself. Letting her guard down when she was pondering her existence, she didn't notice the small shadow above her and was easy prey for the hungry starling. As the bird cracked her shell it dropped her, still alive and she plummeted to earth knowing that her short life as a dung beetle was over.

The hideous hands started poking and prodding and she felt herself being pulled downwards again. Sandy thought she was imagining it when the cruel hands were slowly replaced by soft, gentle ones. She recalled the hands when she had first died and they reminded her of that experience. She quickly put that thought from her mind; assuming that this was just another cruel trick and that if she got comfortable the evil demons would appear and say *April Fool* or something similar. Now there were only gentle hands and Sandy noticed the change in direction. She started to hope against hope that her days with the evils were over. Eventually she allowed herself to relax and enjoy the journey.

*****

Claire didn't know how long she'd been back on the living plain. Every time she'd tried to return to Cherussola, she'd been blocked and had been forced to remain on Earth.

She watched her brothers who didn't appear to be in their usual daily work routine. They were both laughing and joking as each packed a bag too large for one night away.

'I'll take the suits,' said Tony as he picked up the two covered hangers and left the flat whistling a tune that Claire recognized instantly. *I'm getting married in the morning.* But it must have been a coincidence, as Claire knew that Jim and Fiona had promised her mother they'd wait until she returned from Zambia. Although this was her mother's second stint abroad as a volunteer, Fiona wanted a special wedding and they were still saving for the occasion. Claire pondered for a while and decided to hang around to find out what was going on. She heard voices coming from the front door and recognised Fiona's laugh and Libby's high-pitched giggle. She sensed their excitement but still wasn't sure what was happening. They entered the living room and Libby took hold of Tony and gave him a long, lingering kiss, ignoring the presence of his twin and Fiona. When they came up for air Libby's expression turned serious.

'Two days, my love and I'll always be the happiest woman on Earth.'

'You know our mothers won't be very happy?'

They'd had this conversation many times before but Libby still answered patiently. 'My father's not here to give me away and I can't do the big production thing without him. You do understand?'

Tony was still amazed that the death of his sister and Libby's father was the catalyst that had brought both families together. It was small consolation but at least something good had come out of their deaths.

'He might well be watching.'

'Whatever,' said Libby knowing full well that the twins thought they could talk to their dead sister. The twins and Fiona had tried without success to convince her that the siblings could still communicate with each other but Libby was a non-believer. Fiona looked at her friend and hoped that the show she was taking Libby to the following night might change her attitude and make her more open to discussion.

As Claire watched and listened to the conversation the penny dropped. She knew her mother wouldn't be very pleased and assumed that neither would Libby's. Her father wouldn't be happy to miss the wedding either. Now that she knew what was going on she intended to stay and watch the proceedings. She loved a good wedding and was curious to see what sort of do they had chosen. Claire's next thought was one of frustration as she found herself on the cream sofa in Cherussola in front of the beautiful but sometimes irritating angel, Gabriella. Knowing that Gabriella could sense her moods and that she hadn't yet won a battle of wills with the beautiful angel, Claire resisted the urge to complain. She hoped beyond hope that Ron had decided to delay his ascension to heaven and waited with baited breath as her frustration slowly dissipated.

'I have some news,' Gabriella paused to create tension like a seasoned Hollywood actress. I can play that game thought Claire but her mentor knew her for what she was and Claire was the first to break the silence.

'Has Ron decided to stay?'

Gabriella ignored the question. 'I have someone to see you.'

Claire sucked in her breath and waited for Ron to appear. She'd missed him and was so glad he'd decided to stay. She couldn't hide her disappointment when a female image slowly appeared beside her on the sofa. Claire recognised the woman who'd been murdered by her half-sister's captor.

'Hi, I'm Sandy. Pleased to meet you,' she sounds as if she's at a cocktail party or something thought Claire unkindly as she tried not to show her disappointment.

'Hello, Sandy. I was sorry to see the circumstances of your passing,' she attempted a smile but Sandy could see it didn't reach her eyes and she nervously picked at one of the cushions. Claire vowed to get a grip of herself, after all it wasn't the woman's fault that Ron hadn't appeared. Gabriella broke her train of thought.

'I'll leave you ladies to get acquainted. Sandy's been to hell so go easy on her. Back shortly,' she disappeared with her usual whoosh and Sandy smiled ingratiatingly at Claire who thought she looked terrified.

'Ask me anything you want to know and I'll try and explain as best I can,' this time her smile was genuine and Sandy visibly relaxed.

*****

Ron was torn. The unknown delights of heaven were extremely tempting, but he wasn't sure whether he was ready to leave and abrogate all responsibility for Val, his widow. As much as he loved his children, he was confident that they could look after themselves and he knew they'd be able to carve out good lives. It came as something of a shock that Claire was a major reason for his indecision.

Since they'd died she had become something of a substitute daughter and he knew that if he left her permanently, to say she wouldn't be happy was a major understatement.

'That's not your problem.'

Gabriella's voice shook Ron from his reverie and made him jump.

'I wish you wouldn't do that,' she'd sneaked up on him and he'd been so deep in thought that he hadn't heard the customary whoosh.

'I feel responsible for her.'

'Are we talking about Claire or your wife?'

'Both actually,' Ron scratched his chin and was surprised to feel a beard. He raised his eyebrows but Gabriella ignored his silent question, deciding to deal with the more immediate concerns.

'I can't make the decision for you, Ron. But if you have reservations it may mean that now isn't the right time.'

12

The decision was made. He knew the only reason he'd wanted to move up to heaven was curiosity about the pleasures of a wonderful eternity. It wasn't enough and he wasn't yet ready. About to voice his decision, Gabriella spoke before he had a chance.

'Time to tell Claire. Do you want to give her the news or shall I?' now that he'd made up his mind, Ron was eager for her to know.

'I'll go tell her,' he disappeared and Gabriella smiled to herself. Everything had gone as she'd planned. As soon as they were reunited and off to catch up with their families and friends, it would give her time to get Sandy up to speed so that when Ron did decide to go upstairs, Claire would have a ready and willing helper in the wings.

Now free to come and go as she pleased as long as she had Gabriella's permission to do so, Claire decided to return to Earth in time for the wedding. Her brothers and the girls were in the car and Claire saw the sign for Gretna Green, the first village in Scotland, and chuckled to herself. So they were marrying in the village where young English people used to run away to marry years before when the marriage laws of Scotland allowed, but England did not. Claire appreciated Libby's sense of humour but the thought of their wedding made her feel nostalgic. Although she'd come to terms with the fact that she no longer had Jay and was happy that he'd found someone else, seeing her brothers happy with their partners made her realise how lonely she was, and she was also incredibly bored.

'Fancy some company?'

It was a moment before she realised that Ron was speaking to her and she did a double take, clapping her hands together and laughing as he materialized. Claire enveloped him in a tight hug that made Ron lose his balance.

'Steady, girl.'

'Does this mean…'

'Yup. I've decided that someone needs to keep an eye on you so I'm going to be around for a while yet.'

She leaned back from him but still held him at arms length. He could see that she was trying to say something but couldn't form the words. She eventually gave up and hugged him again, this time even tighter, and Ron felt the wetness from her tears on the back of his shoulder.

'Thank you. Oh, Ron. Thank you so much for staying, I…'

'There, there,' was all he could manage as he rubbed her back until she regained control of her emotions. Eventually they broke apart and Claire gave a self-conscious laugh before deciding it was down to business. It always amazed him how she could change from being super emotional one minute, to so business-like the next. She explained what had been happening while he'd been making his mind up and how she'd helped her brothers solve a number of criminal cases.

'What has Libby got to say about all of this?'

Ron was eager to hear news of his daughter. The last he'd heard, the relationship between Tony and Libby was getting quite serious.

'Well,' said Claire and Ron could tell from her tone that she was dying to impart some important news.

'What? Just tell me.'

'Do you know where we are?'

They'd only just reunited and she was beginning to irritate him already.

'Spill, Claire. And now.'

'They're getting married in Gretna Green. Tomorrow or the day after, I'm not sure which.'

'What!'

'I said…'

'I know what you said, Claire. But why Gretna Green? Did Val and your mother come home early then?'

Claire explained that both mothers were still in Zambia and that Libby wanted a quiet affair because her father wasn't there to give her away. Ron was thoughtful for a moment. Quietly taking in the information he shook his head.

'Val's going to be very upset and so is your mother. I'm glad I got back in time to see her though. I'd like to find a way to show her I'm watching over her.'

Ron couldn't communicate with the living but Claire could ensure that her brothers knew they were there.

'But that won't convince Libby, you know how stubborn she can be.'

Claire knew only too well. When Tony had first tried explaining her presence to Libby it had freaked her and she couldn't handle it. As time passed she'd come to accept that the twins gained some sort of comfort from talking to their dead sister though Libby had stubbornly refused to believe that they actually communicated with her, despite their assertions as well as Fiona's. Tony had asked Claire to stay away when Libby was around and she'd reluctantly agreed to do so. A nudge from Ron broke her train of thought.

'I certainly do but I have an idea. And if it all goes to plan, Ron, Libby will know that her Daddy is watching over her.' Claire smiled smugly and Ron found himself extremely curious but irritated by her for the second time within a matter of minutes.

Chapter 2

He sighed contentedly as the young girl lifted herself off him and slowly put on her underwear and the faded shift dress. She was stunning. Dark chocolate skin as smooth as a baby's and a beautiful lithe body though underfed and not yet fully developed. They'd trained her well and he smiled guiltily as he remembered the sensations he'd felt when she'd used that skilful full mouth to pleasure his body. He looked at her beautiful deep brown eyes. Eyes that were completely dead to him, but he chose not to notice. He didn't know how old she was, they were usually very young, and he'd only used her because he made sure these girls were clean but he always felt guilty afterwards. He preferred grown women but didn't want to chance going with a diseased prostitute. He'd pleasured himself for months but eventually gave in to his need of a female body. Before he'd got into trouble in England he'd been a supplier rather than a user of younger women and he reflected how his life had changed. In some ways it was a lot better. He liked his new look and every time he stared at his reflection, couldn't help a little grin. He was better than the men he supplied with the young girls, but wouldn't show them that – why bite the hands that feed you? Old job but in a new country, new name, new face, hell perhaps it was the time to get a new woman! Gary closed his eyes and thought about the English women at the orphanage. One was crusty and he'd have to work hard to charm her, but the other had definitely had a spark in her eyes and they'd hit it off from the start. If he played his cards right...

Tamara looked at the man on the bed who was smiling to himself with his eyes closed. For her part she knew it wasn't her place to ask for anything in return for satisfying him and she also knew that her face looked older than her 12 years. She'd aged since being taken away from the home and from knowing that she existed purely for the pleasure of sick older men. The few people that had cared thought her dead and this had been explained to her. Her face lacked hope and she knew that if she didn't perform for her rich masters, they would make her life miserable. She tried to comfort herself by thinking she had more than some. They fed her well and her surroundings were comfortable. She also had the company of friends who were in the same situation and life could be fun when she wasn't forced to go with these men. But no matter how much she tried to convince herself that things could be worse, her soul ached from the depravations placed upon it.

*****

Val and Marion were coming to the end of the fourth month of their second stint in Zambia. The orphanage had been completed during their first tour and Marion walked around a bend in the dirt road and the modest buildings of the orphanage came into view. The one-storey school building stood to the right and a larger two-storey where they lived and ate to the left. The communal rooms downstairs consisted of an eating area, a small medical room and separate washing and toilet areas for boys and girls. The Ministry of Community Development and their charity, People Against Poverty had recently completed the water project, which resulted in water being pumped into a well from a bore hole. The pump had the capacity to work to a depth of 85 metres and both the orphans and staff were grateful and felt lucky to be able to use a daily ration of 7.5 litres of this much sought after fluid. Basic sleeping accommodation was upstairs, again separated for boys and girls and each child had a space that contained their own small bed, meagre belongings and the luxury of a mosquito net. The orphanage accommodated 102 children aged between 9 and 13; 52 boys and 50 girls.

Marion frowned at the memory of the two girls who had died. She'd been given the news along with Val and the other two volunteers, and little other information. When she'd asked to see the bodies to say goodbye to the children her request had been refused and Marion was still upset by the deaths. Daniel, one of the newer members of staff, had been acting as Assistant Coordinator since Thomas had left to oversee the building of a new orphanage near Lusaka. Both Marion and Val had got along well with Thomas but not so his successor. They realised that his inexperience might make him defensive but couldn't understand the cold and seemingly uncaring and matter of fact way in which he'd announced the deaths of the two girls. It had affected all the children and the other staff had upped their efforts to make the children feel safe. Marion and Val had noticed that the local staff behaved differently around Daniel and they'd already decided to speak to the charity about his appointment on their return to London. In the meantime they'd resigned themselves to the fact that they had to get on with him as best they could and try not to let his attitude interfere with running the orphanage and educating the children.

Along with the five children who she'd taken with her to collect water from the well, she turned to the sound of a vehicle approaching from behind and smiled falsely as the big white man driving the Land Rover lifted a hand from the steering wheel and waved. He was very good-looking and charismatic and Marion had no idea why, when she'd first met him, the hairs on the back of her neck stood up and her gut instinct told her not to trust the man. He'd evoked the opposite reaction in Val and they'd flirted openly on the three occasions they'd met. Marion knew that Gary's firm supplied the building materials for the charity at reduced cost so she had to be polite, but that didn't mean she had to like him. She had no idea why he needed to visit today so upped her pace towards the front door and two of the smaller children had to run to keep up with her.

*****

It was the evening before the wedding and Libby was feeling a little nervous. Her brother Carl had arrived to be a guest and witness and though he knew their mother would be upset that Libby had married without her present, he also knew that she'd be over the moon to see her daughter happy again, eventually. Carl had gone off with Jim and Tony, and Libby and Tony had decided that they wouldn't see each other until the ceremony the following day.

'What have you got planned for us this evening?' Libby was curious as Fiona had said it would be a surprise. She'd already had a low-key hen night the previous week with Fiona and six of her other close friends and didn't want a boozy night before her wedding the following day. When she'd said this to Fiona a few weeks previously, Fiona had told her not to worry and that she'd arrange something to keep the pre-wedding nerves at bay.

'So come on then, what are we doing?' Fiona hadn't answered the question and Libby was very curious.

'Actually, it's a surprise. We leave in half an hour and there's no need to dress up.'

'What sort of surprise?'

'You'll find out when we get there.'

Claire and Ron had heard the entire conversation and both were as curious as Libby. They didn't have long to wait.

19

The disused cinema in the town had been converted into a Bingo Hall but also doubled as a venue for presentations, shows and concerts. The taxi pulled up and Fiona and Libby got out, Libby still not knowing what Fiona had planned. Her friend dragged her quickly into the building's foyer and Libby assumed they had come to see a local play. Not giving her an opportunity to stop and look around, Fiona pulled her arm and led her into the main room, after showing a woman on the entrance door their tickets. She walked towards the stage at the front of the room and ushered Libby into the second seat from the end. Libby decided to play the game, it was a little exciting not knowing what was going on, but only until the host walked onto the stage and made the announcement.

'Ladies and gentlemen, her fame has spread throughout the length and breadth of the United Kingdom, she's brought comfort to countless people who've lost loved ones, and hope to many others,' he paused. Fiona looked at Libby and didn't see any recognition on her face. Good, she thought, she hasn't clicked yet.

'Ladies and gentlemen, Gretna is proud to welcome Delores Davies for a night with the dead.'

The audience rose to their feet and applauded as a pink-haired middle-aged woman dressed from head to toe in pink, walked onto the stage holding open her arms in invitation.

'I'm out of here,' Libby couldn't believe that Fiona had brought her to this farcical show. Fiona held her arm in a vice-like grip and pulled her back into her seat. The rest of the audience had calmed down by this stage and Delores got straight into her work.

'Is there someone here who's lost a son called Davy or maybe David? He's holding his neck in an unusual way. I get a feeling of a major impact, maybe a car accident?'

'That's my boy,' shouted a woman from the audience.

'Oh my God,' said Libby before putting her head in her hands and shaking it. 'I don't bloody believe you've brought me here.'

'It might actually change your views and teach you to be more open minded,' Fiona replied, but as she watched Libby sit up straight and fold her arms she very much doubted her own words.

'Was this your plan, to talk to her through this medium person?' Ron asked Claire while looking around the hall. He could see that there weren't any other departed souls present and wondered how the woman was receiving messages.

'No. I was going to speak through Jim when Fiona and Libby were there but Tony wasn't. Anyway, it looks like we've lucked out,' she could see that Ron was baffled. 'She's obviously a fake, Ron and has planted people in the audience.'

It was obvious now that Claire had explained and they watched for a few minutes as Delores went to two other people in the audience. Claire was becoming increasingly annoyed at the pretender on the stage and tried her best to talk to the woman, but there was nothing there. Just as they decided it was time to leave the door opened and a man walked down the aisle toward the stage. Claire and Ron gasped. They'd never seen so many dead souls, all talking at the same time and plainly driving the man to distraction. Above the souls who were buzzing around the man in an attempt to get his attention, was a male angel. Claire's jaw hung open at his stunning good looks, beautiful black skin and soulful dark eyes which looked as if they were deep in concentration dealing with the hellish souls that he didn't want to get through to the genuine Medium. Some he pushed away and with others he had to work a little harder. They saw the teenage spirit who had tried causing trouble for their own families and the beautiful angel gave him what appeared to be a gentle shove. The teenager screamed and disappeared into the ether like a comet shooting through the night sky. The angel looked directly at Ron and Claire and winked. He appeared to up the ante when he realised he had an audience. Typical man thought Claire but was mesmerized by his graceful movements. She thought he looked like a heavenly dark Jackie Chan as he fought off the evil spirits sometimes four or five at a time. There were a few seconds where the angel had the opportunity to take stock and he beckoned to Claire and Ron. They rushed to his side and he spoke.

'Good evening. My name is Raphael and I work with Gabriella,' he had a voice that Claire could listen to all day and made her want to eat chocolate. His looks matched his voice, dark and mysterious but not as dark as Gabriella. When he looked directly at her his eyes seemed to melt her soul and she felt as if she could stare into them for eternity. Ron broke the spell.

'We're pleased to meet you. How can we help?'

Claire shook herself and stopped daydreaming.

Raphael wondered why he couldn't read Claire. He had important work to do and would have to think about that when time allowed. Rubbing his hands together he gave his instructions.

'When I give the command, hold my hands and we'll form a circle. Concentrate on everything good that happened when you were alive, the love you shared with others and good deeds that you did. If a bad thought tries to surface, push it away gently. Most of them can't get through as long as we're bathed in love,' Raphael closed his eyes and continued. 'If this works I'll reward you with faster access to the Medium, Claire and you'll be able to pass Ron's message to his daughter,' he held out his hands and they linked. Claire tingled with sensations she hadn't felt since...

'But can't I talk to the Medium like the other spirits are doing?' Ron took back a hand and pointed to the mass of souls chattering away to the poor man who was seemingly trying to block out all of the noise as he strode purposefully to the stage.

'You certainly could, Ron. But you know that Claire has more power than you and with my help her voice will stand out amongst the others. I feel a new wave of evils approaching, let's get on and remember what I told you.'

They forgot about what was going on in the show as all their efforts were concentrated on blocking out the evil spirits.

Michael Gray was not a happy man. He was fed up with charlatans making money out of the grief and misery of others and determined to do something about it. He looked at the woman on the stage with disgust. He'd been to one of her shows before just to make sure and knew for a fact that she was a fake. Nobody expected trouble at this type of event and Michael knew that it would take a little while before any of the staff would think to phone the police or some sort of security personnel. He wasn't even sure that they employed security staff. He jumped onto the stage, barely acknowledging Delores and smiled at the audience. It was important to get them on side as soon as possible. The last thing he needed was a *have a go hero* from the audience trying to tackle him.

'Good evening, ladies and gentlemen,' he waited until the muttering had stopped and he had their full attention. 'My name's Michael and I apologise for the inconvenience but I have a number of messages here for some of you and I wanted to make sure that you receive them,' there was deathly silence and looking down, Michael put his hands to the side of his head.

'All right, all right. One of you at a time,' he smiled and looked up. 'Kay Beattie, that top's far too low cut and yellow is most certainly not your colour.'

A woman stood up blushing bright red. 'Err, who told you that?'

'Doreen,' said Michael. 'She's an older lady dressed very conservatively...' he stopped as if listening to someone. 'She passed almost a year ago and said to tell you that she's reunited with Albert and that although your choice of clothing is dubious, your man is the right choice and they're looking forward to seeing the little one.'

Kay put her hand to her mouth and the woman in the chair next to her started crying. 'You're pregnant?' said the woman between tears.

'Yes, Ma.'

The two hugged and the audience clapped, won over by Michael's message and, for the moment, forgetting about Delores.

'Thank you so much,' said Kay, but her words were drowned out by the applause.

'I think it's time to leave, young man,' Delores was now on her feet and approaching Michael.

'This woman's a fake,' he shouted as he jumped down from the stage and made for the exit. 'I have an important message for Libby. It's from a friend of your father and he wants you to know that he'll be at your wedding tomorrow.'

As the crowd chanted his name and Michael ran to the exit, dodging staff members as he did, Libby's mouth gaped open and Fiona nodded with a smug told you so expression on her face. Libby jumped to her feet and grabbed Fiona and they both ran out of the room, hot on the heels of Michael Gray.

Chapter 3

Fiona and Libby had breakfasted together on the morning of the wedding. Libby was in the hotel's salon flicking through a magazine while the stylist fussed with her hair. Fiona had expected her to be nervous and emotional but Libby was calm and happy.

'Knowing that Dad's okay wherever he is has made so much difference,' she put down the magazine. 'And that he's going to be at my wedding. I'm so happy, Fi.' Unable to hug her friend due to the stylist's ministrations, Fiona held Libby's hand and gave it a squeeze.

'The only ones who know about the song my father used to sing to me in the garden are my mother and brother, and there's no way they could have told Michael. I can't wait to give my mother her message as well. It'll be like a weight's been lifted,' she picked up the magazine again. 'Why don't you leave me to it and I'll text you when I'm done.'

It was the excuse Fiona needed to get away for a while. She hadn't seen Jim since the events of the previous evening and was dying to tell the twins what the Medium had said. She also hoped they'd be able to get hold of a special song to make Libby's day even better.

'Okay if you're absolutely sure?'

Libby nodded and Fiona lifted her phone out of her pocket, texting Jim as she left the salon.

'So you're telling me that Libby's father gave Claire a message to give to this Michael bloke, and he gave a message to Libby?' asked Jim as the four were walking in the hotel grounds.

'My father gave my sister a message through a Medium?'

'Yes, and yes,' replied Fiona. She could see that Carl looked sceptical. 'Remember the song *It's a Wonderful World?*' That showed him she thought as his expression turned to one of disbelief.

'He used to sing that to her in the garden when she was a kid.'

'Uhh, huh.'

'But nobody would know about that.'

'Uhh, huh.'

Fiona noticed the knowing look between the twins, remembering how shocked she'd been when she realised that their sister was really able to communicate with them. The group remained quiet as Carl digested the information. A gentle gust of wind blew a few rose petals along the path in front of them and Fiona hoped that the weather would remain dry for the ceremony and the few photographs afterward.

'I can't believe it.'

'Not you as well,' he can be as stubborn as his sister thought Fiona. 'Look, I know it's hard to take in but I can only tell you what the Medium said and how Libby reacted. Let's just concentrate on the wedding and try to get the song played at the ceremony,' she turned to Tony. 'Would you be okay with that?'

'If it makes Libby happy I'm fine with that.'

'Good, because I've already downloaded it and sorted it with the Registrar.'

Another look passed between the twins. They knew what a bossy go-getter Fiona could be when the need arose. She preferred to think of herself as having second to none leadership and organisational abilities.

*****

Marion reached the building to hear Val and the visitor laughing.

'Hello, Marion. How are you?' he gave her his best smile.

'Fine thanks. You?' the smile wasn't returned.

'Just leaving actually. See you later, Val.'

'Will do.'

She sounded like a teenager to Marion who raised her eyebrows after Gary had left.

'It's just a bit of fun. He's taking me for a drive later to see some of the wildlife, you can come if you want.'

'No thanks.' Marion put down the water and asked the children to take it to the kitchen. 'There's something not right about him, Val. I wish you wouldn't.'

'Don't worry about me. It's only a bit of harmless fun. Why don't you come with us you're always saying you wish you could see some of the animals?' Val was grateful her friend had looked after her when she'd been attacked. She was getting fed-up with Marion's over-protectiveness though, which was stilting her independence, and if she wasn't careful they were likely to fall out.

'Shall we have a quick cup of tea?' Marion tried a different tack explaining to Val that she wanted to talk to her about a dream she'd had the previous night. This was the first time they'd seen each other that morning and she was keen to have a chat.

Marion carefully poured the water into the mugs, ensuring there was no spill and used one tea bag between them. They'd got used to black tea on their first tour and didn't blink an eye as they sipped at the thick, bitter liquid.

'It seemed so real that I have to tell you. And it's been ages since I've had such a vivid dream.'

'Sounds intriguing,' said Val.

'First of all I dreamt that Tony and your Libby got married.'

'They haven't known each long enough yet!' Val laughed.

'Then I dreamt that your husband said that Gary's a bad one and you should leave well alone.' Marion took a deep breath knowing that Val wouldn't like what she'd said. But she was her friend and she had to tell her, even though she knew Val wouldn't be happy.

'Below the belt, Marion.' Val pushed back her chair and stood up. 'I can't spend all day chatting. I've got work to do.'

'But Val..'

'I don't want to fall out with you, Marion but I like Gary and it's only a bit of fun. You're thinking of things before you go to sleep and your sub-conscious is trying to work it out while you're sleeping. But just because you don't like him it doesn't mean to say that I don't and acting as if Ron has sent a message is just plain cruel.' Val stormed off without bothering to wait for a reply. Marion regretted falling out with her friend but hadn't regretted telling her, such was the strength of her uneasiness when in Gary's presence.

*****

Libby looked gorgeous in her tight fitting knee-length white dress patterned with red and yellow roses. She walked along the red carpet, arms linked with her brother and this image of his beautiful bride would be in Tony's memory forever.

The wedding was taking place in *The Old Blacksmith's Shop* a traditional place for ceremonies since the 18th century when youngsters could be legally married in Scotland, but not in England and Wales. Such was the popularity of the place that people from all over the world married there. It was a beautiful village but obvious to the wedding party that wedding tourism was the major income generator. Libby felt a slight tinge of guilt that her mother wasn't there. She vowed to herself that they would celebrate with a party when her mother returned from Zambia – she'd always said that she didn't want a big ceremony and now hoped her mother had taken her seriously. The sight of her groom made any negative thoughts disappear and Libby was constantly amazed at how quickly she'd found her soul mate.

They exchanged vows and Libby cried tears of both joy and sadness when *What a Wonderful World* played as they signed the register to formalise their union. She looked heavenward.

'Thanks, Dad. I know you're there and that you're okay now,' Fiona handed Libby a cotton handkerchief. She wiped her eyes and smiled self-consciously at the small group of family and friends and the Registrar, before looking up again. 'I miss you, Dad and I'll always love you.'

There wasn't a dry eye amongst the living at the ceremony, or the dead onlookers.

The twins knew that Claire was with them but had chosen not to mention it. They were not yet fully confident that Libby was ready to accept their dead sister into their daily lives. Her speech to her father had shown them all that she was now a believer but Tony still wondered how his wife would react if he had a conversation with his sister in her presence. He put the thought out of his mind. This was his wedding day and was about his beautiful bride, not his sadly departed and sometimes very irritating sister.

Libby's emotions were all over the place. They'd had a lovely lunch following their wedding and the others had disappeared shortly after, giving them a chance to consummate their vows. The suite was absolutely beautiful. Libby had planned for them to share some champagne in the Jacuzzi so they could chat while taking in the views of the rolling Scottish countryside. As it happened they couldn't keep their hands off each other. It wouldn't have made a difference whether they'd been in their current bridal suite or a farmyard barn; they only had eyes for each other. Exhausted from their passionate lovemaking they slept for a while, and Libby's pleasure centre had woken her when her husband's kisses and hands told her it was time for more. Much later they showered and dressed and decided on a walk by the river.

'I'm so happy,' she said and he squeezed her hand and smiled in acknowledgement, not needing to comment until he sensed there was more.

'There sounds like a but, Libby?'

'I wish my mother had been at the wedding.'

Tony attempted a comment but Libby put a finger to his lips. 'If I hadn't known about my father everything would have been fine. He was there so my mother should have been.'

'Come here.' Tony embraced his wife and resisted the urge to say I told you. It was an understatement to say that his mother would be unhappy at missing their wedding and he'd tried to talk Libby out of doing it this way, but she'd been adamant so he'd reluctantly gone along with her. His father had a competition but said he would have gladly withdrawn from it but Tony knew that his mother would be even more upset if she'd discovered his father had attended but she had not. For his own part Tony was just happy they were together and the future would work itself out.

They walked on in silence for a while, seeing the occasional water vole scurry across the muddy riverside, alarmed by their presence in the otherwise peaceful surroundings.

'Why don't we do it all again when they return and not tell them about this one?' said Tony and his wife laughed, startling a pair of ducks that quacked and pedalled along the water in preparation for flight.

He'd do anything to make her happy and Libby felt blessed. She had to take responsibility though and do the right thing.

'How about we all go away somewhere for a long weekend when they get back, and have some sort of blessing or formal ceremony?'

Tony stopped to think for a moment.

'Well? How does that sound?'

'Providing our mothers are still speaking to us once they've found out what we've done, I think it's a good idea, but I'm not sure how that would work with my father being there.'

Libby hadn't thought that their mothers would be that annoyed and hoped that his parents could put their differences aside for their son's sake, for just one day.

'Look at that,' Tony pointed to the beautiful blue of a kingfisher that had caught his eye and they watched the bird dive into the water, retrieve a fish and fly away.

They forgot about their parents as they took in the beauty and savagery of nature around them and enjoyed the rest of their stroll.

*****

As Marion and Val had enjoyed their tea but not each other's company, Daniel had been summoned by Gary and he walked out into the bush with the Englishman. There was nobody else about to hear them.

'I want the tall one with the oval face. What did her parents die of?'

Knowing that HIV and AIDS was prevalent in Zambia and one of the major reasons for the large number of orphans, Gary was always careful when choosing his next sex slave victims.

'I'll check her medical records,' said Daniel, 'but it may take a few days.' His appointment meant that he had access to records of all the children, but would have to ask the clerk to take out the file. This

31

could well cause suspicion when the girl went missing, even though the police investigation would be cursory.

'Not good enough, my friend,' the words sent a shiver up Daniel's spine and he avoided looking into Gary's eyes, frightened at what the man would make him do.

'I'm taking Val out later on, and when her friend takes some of them to get water this evening, I want you to make sure the girl doesn't go if she was due to go with them?'

Daniel nodded and Gary continued.

'You will arrange for her to go out via the back door.'

Daniel started to protest but Gary silenced him with a look.

'Then one of my men will grab her. You'll be in the clear as long as you can think of a believable excuse for her to go outside. But before all that, go and check her medical documents. Comprende?'

He understood all right and he also realised that the Englishman was willing to take more and more risks. However, his lifestyle had improved since he'd been helping Gary and at least these girls were getting decent accommodation, not like those orphans living on the streets of the capital and having to prostitute themselves just to get food. Daniel's warped reasoning helped him to justify his actions and he knew deep down that he'd do anything to be able to keep the luxuries to which his family had become accustomed. His wife treated him with respect these days and that alone was worth the risk.

Chapter 4

It was Val's afternoon off and she hastily dragged a comb through her hair when she heard the Land Rover pull up outside the staff accommodation. She checked her appearance in the cracked piece of mirror leaning up against the old, uneven dressing table. She'd accumulated a few more wrinkles since working in Zambia and her roots could do with a touch up, but under the circumstances she was content with her looks. Losing Ron almost two years before had aged her but she was finally starting to get her mojo back and wanted to play a bit as well as work hard. She hadn't been with another man since the dreadful time of Ron and Ken's death and the memory of her guilt back then made her frown. She'd admitted to herself that she missed physical contact and was ready for a bit of fun, but certainly wasn't ready for another long-term relationship. Val didn't know if she'd ever be ready for that. She wondered if Marion ever missed having a sex life. They'd talked about many things during their friendship but Marion's sex life wasn't one of them and Val wondered, cruelly, if Marion didn't like Gary because he was interested in her and not Marion. Jealousy would explain why Marion had made such unkind comments that were so out of character. Val knew to trust her own instincts, especially after the attack the previous year and she didn't get any bad vibes when she was with Gary. In fact, he'd acted like the perfect gentleman.

The beeping horn brought her back to the present and she put her hair in a ponytail and ran down the wooden stairs. She stopped and composed herself at the bottom not wishing to appear too keen.

They laughed and chatted on the journey. Val knew that the nature reserve was too far to travel there and back in an afternoon, but Gary had said that they might see some elephant and antelope. He added that if they were really lucky and very quiet, their patience might be rewarded with the sight of a leopard. Val was used to the bumpy roads and tracks around the orphanage area and to and from the market, but once off the beaten track things were even worse. Gary had explained that part of the ride would be slow going, but she hadn't taken the discomfort into consideration. They'd been travelling at a snail's pace for over an hour when Val asked for a break.

'I think my back's going to break in two, Gary. Any chance...'

A loud growling roar in the distance cut off her voice. The sound sent shivers up her spine and Gary stopped the vehicle and looked around. They saw the big cat halfway up a tree. It had laid down its small prey and turned its fierce eyes on the vehicle and its occupants. Val was both fascinated and terrified. Gary reversed very slowly and the animal appeared to relax a little, but not enough for Val's liking.

'Like any animal, they're at their most dangerous when protecting their food or their young. I don't like the look of this one so we're going to go back in the direction we came and find another route. Okay?'

She nodded while keeping her eyes on the leopard. She knew that Gary had a gun with him and wondered if the leopard took a jump at them, would he choose to drive or to stop and use the gun. She needn't have worried as the animal continued its feast when it could see that they were no longer a threat and Val was soon able to relax a little. When they arrived at a shaded area a while later Gary stopped the Land Rover and smiled.

'Are you okay?' he asked, eyes full of concern as he leaned over and patted her thigh.

His hand stayed there a second too long and Val felt herself blush as memories of being touched by a red-blooded male flooded her mind. It made her think of Ron but strangely enough she didn't feel guilty. She looked upwards and smiled.

'Val?'

'Yes I'm fine thanks. That was a bit scary though.'

Gary laughed and Val got the impression that her idea of scary and his were entirely different.

'Can you give me a hand?' he got out of the vehicle and Val followed him around to the back where he untied the canopy that was covering the boot. Gary unstrapped the bungee cords that were holding a cool box in place and lifted the box. He handed her the blanket that was underneath and walked to the rear passenger seats where his rifle was stored. 'Insurance,' he said giving her a charming smile and set off carrying the box and rifle. Val followed and they stopped at a nearby tree, which was on a slight hill. Gary appeared to survey the area and once satisfied nodded his head for Val to lay the blanket. They sat down and looked around. It was a stunning vista of hills in the distance that seemed to end abruptly. Gary pointed and explained that the steep hillside plunged down into a deep ravine and that he'd take her there on their next outing. Val ignored his presumption that they'd have another outing and looked at their surroundings. In their immediate line of sight the open grassy plains were dotted with an occasional tree. They could see for miles and would be able to spot any potential danger long before it reached them.

'Nothing too fancy I'm afraid,' Gary opened the box and took out two cans of coke. 'We'll let them settle for a few minutes before opening them.' He took out two foil packages and passed her one. 'Hope you like the local ham.'

Val nodded gratefully, pleased with his thoughtfulness as he must have guessed that she hadn't had time for lunch prior to his arrival.

Shaded under the tree they ate and drank in comfortable silence for a while, taking in the views and the grazing animals. Val hadn't felt this relaxed for some time and she closed her eyes after she'd finished eating. There were unknown dangers out here but she felt completely safe in the company of the big charming man beside her. She wasn't sure how much later it was when she felt his hand on her arm and his voice brought her back to the present.

'Sorry to wake you but I think we'd better make a move.'

Val opened her eyes and stretched like a lazy cat. Looking up she was surprised to see that the sun had moved a distance from its zenith.

'How long have I been out of it?'

Gary laughed before replying. 'At least a couple of hours. You must have been really tired.'

'But I thought we were going to try and get nearer to the Reserve?'

'I'm sorry, but I didn't want to disturb you.'

He looked disappointed and Val felt ungrateful. He was being thoughtful and she had implied criticism at his decision.

'Thanks, Gary. Maybe another day then?'

They both knew this wasn't a one-off and gathered their belongings to put back into the Land Rover. Ready to leave, Gary was about to put the key in the ignition when Val spoke.

'Thanks so much for today. I've really enjoyed myself and didn't realise how much I needed to get away from the orphanage for a while,' she leaned toward him and gave him a quick peck on the cheek. Val was almost as surprised as Gary and blushed at her own impulsiveness. She wound down her window and looked out, studying the countryside intently so she didn't have to look at the big man beside her.

He turned the key in the ignition and the engine coughed but nothing happened. Gary tried again and again and Val eventually turned back to look at him, her earlier blushes put aside for the time being as she realised what was happening.

'Problem?'

'Yup,' he got out and fiddled with a few things under the bonnet. 'Try the ignition again, Val.'

She leaned over and turned the key with the same result. He closed the bonnet and walked to the passenger side of the vehicle. 'We have a problem.'

*****

The afternoon was flying by and it was time to collect some more water. Daniel had asked Marion if she'd go again as he wanted to catch up on some paperwork, so she gathered the children together but noticed they were one short.

'Where's Mary?' Mary was a beautiful girl not yet a teenager, but with a teenage attitude. Marion could forgive her the bad attitude and most other things for that matter. None of the orphans had had an easy time of it and Mary was no exception. Her parents, brother and sister had been murdered in a tribal killing. Mary had been wounded and was forced to lie under their bodies until a long time after the attackers had left. She had scars on her side and back from the gun wounds but had fought for survival. She was understandably wary about getting close to anyone and for the most part, kept her emotions veiled. Marion had seen her smile a few times recently but knew that she would carry the emotional scars with her for the rest of her life. She sent one of the children to get Mary; a few minutes later the girl came back with a message.

'Daniel says she's not well so he's sent her to bed and Nursie will see her later.'

Marion frowned. It was unusual for Daniel to be so sympathetic. The children generally had to be seen by the nurse before he showed any concern. Mary had plenty of psychological problems but was physically robust unlike many of the other children. The pulling at Marion's t-shirt forced her to look at the smiling little face.

'Are we going, Missy?'

'We certainly are, Suria,' the child took Marion's hand and started swinging it back and forth as they made their way to the water.

Mary was lying on her bed studying a science textbook. There weren't many books and the children had to share them but luckily for Mary not many were interested in science so she'd been able to keep hold of the book for a few days. She held it as if it were a precious gem and was in awe of the illustrations and explanations within it. She wasn't sure what she wanted to do as a grown up but was very bright so thought she might like to be a doctor. She knew she had to work hard and that her family were watching over her. She wanted to make them very proud, especially her father who had taught them all to be independent and not to expect anything for nothing. She also knew that eventually she'd have to be more trusting of people, but Mary couldn't quite bring herself to trust anyone yet, though she did like some more than others. Daniel came into the room and Mary felt an involuntary shiver. Her father had also told her to trust her instincts and there was something about Daniel that she didn't like. He'd been perfectly pleasant to her and hadn't done anything to make her wary, but she was going to follow her father's advice and she looked at him as he approached her with, Mary thought, a false smile on his face. He'd sent her to the room earlier and told her to expect a surprise and Mary felt she hadn't had any choice but to follow his direction. She enjoyed going to the well with the other children, especially if the white women were accompanying them, but given the choice of learning or going for water then learning would always win. She reluctantly closed the book and sat up on the bed.

'Are you ready for your surprise?' Daniel put out his hand and Mary thought he seemed a bit nervous. She hesitated.

'Come on,' he said reaching for her hand and she put her hand in his and moved to the door with him but something made her hold back.

'What is it?'

Daniel could see that she didn't trust anyone and had not expected her to accompany him on her own without an explanation.

'We're getting you all a pet to share, and you, Mary, are going to be the first to see it!'

Her twelve-year-old mind was working overtime. If they had a cat or a dog she'd be able to talk to it about what happened and nobody else would know. She would love it and it would love her and make her happy again. She hoped it was a dog.

'What is it?' Mary forgot about not trusting Daniel in her excitement.

'Why don't you go out the back and see, they're just about to deliver him.'

Mary ran down the stairs. It was a busy time of day and everybody else was occupied with their own personal chores. She ran out of the back door and saw the old white vehicle. A smiling man opened the door and beckoned her over. She ran to the vehicle hoping there was a dog inside. By the time her young brain realised there was no pet it was too late. She struggled as much as she could but the two men easily overcame her and a smelly rag was forced over her nose and mouth. She stopped struggling when the drug took effect and she was rolled into a blanket and put onto the back seat.

Marion heard a vehicle and thought it must be Val returning from her outing with the creep, as she unkindly thought of him. She was surprised to see the tatty white van go past and wondered what business they'd had at the orphanage. There weren't any food deliveries due that day and as far as Marion knew, only Gary's company worked at the orphanage and she couldn't recall seeing a white van belonging to them. She tried to put it out of her mind but unscheduled visits were unusual so she decided to ask Daniel on her return.

*****

'Can you fix it?' Val knew the answer by the look on Gary's face but asked anyway.

'No. The fuel pump appears to be broken.'

She started to switch off as soon as he mentioned something that she didn't have a clue about. To Val is was the same as when asking a stranger for directions, any more than two instructions and her mind was away with the fairies. Both directions and vehicle parts had exactly the same effect.

'Val?'

'Oh. Do we start walking then?'

Gary laughed at her naivety. 'It's going to be dark in an hour and there's plenty of wildlife here, so no we don't walk anywhere.'

It was just starting to sink in but in case there was any doubt in her mind he added. 'We stay here overnight and hopefully they'll send a vehicle out to find us at first light.'

'Hopefully?'

'No, they will send one. We just have to stay in the Land Rover tonight. We've enough water to last and I always keep some dry rations in the event of an

40

emergency,' he was talking to himself as much as to Val but she was nodding and thinking that it wouldn't be that bad and it was, after all, only one night. They could get to know each other, but definitely not in a physical way.

'Are you all right?'

She answered yes and he suggested that they stay out of the vehicle until just before darkness fell. 'It's going to be cramped in there and once we're in, it's best that we stay there all night.'

'But what if I need the loo?'

'I'll need to escort you, Val and bring the rifle. We'll dig a small trench now at the other side of the tree so we don't have to walk far from the Rover.'

*****

They were about to gather for dinner and Marion wanted a quick word with Daniel before they sat down. She also wanted to check on Mary.

She popped her head around the office door. He was sitting at the old desk, flicking through a file and frowning. He didn't notice her.

'How's Mary.'

He jumped in the seat and looked to Marion as if he'd been caught with his hand in the sweetie jar.

'You made me jump.'

'Clearly. What are you doing?'

'Working hard, obviously.' He closed the file before she had a chance to see what he'd been looking at and put it in one of the desk drawers. Closing the drawer he locked it and put the key in his trouser pocket.

'So, Mary?' Marion repeated, her fingers tapping against the door.

Daniel didn't answer straight away and Marion wondered if he wound her up on purpose. He eventually shrugged his shoulders.

41

'Marion, you may have noticed that I am very busy. Once I sent her to lie down I decided to ask the nurse to check on her after dinner. We'll see if she eats. If she does we'll know that she's not ill and there will be no need to waste the nurse's time.'

Marion wondered what he was hiding, but let it go for the time being.

'Who were the visitors?'

Daniel put down the pen he'd been holding and sighed heavily. 'What?'

'The visitors in the white van. Who were they?'

'Marion. I repeat. I'm very busy. One of the reasons I asked you to do the water detail was so that I could get this paperwork done. I'm going to be working late into the night as it is. I also...'

'But you must have heard the van, even it you didn't see it?'

'I've been immersed in my work and haven't seen or heard anything else,' he stopped her next interruption by adding. 'New volunteers are arriving the week after next, you and Val will be going home early,' he smiled. 'Now shall we go and eat or do you want to hear the rest of it?'

Marion momentarily forgot about Mary as Daniel explained that the charity wanted her and Val to take the lead on a new orphanage being built in Romania. If they agreed, it would mean another course in London. If they were up for it the plan would be to handover to the two new volunteers, return to the UK, have some time off and then attend the course. It was a promotion and Marion was taken aback at the suddenness of the move. She knew before discussing it with Val that this is what she'd aspired to and she would take the job, whether Val wanted to or not. Probably another unkind thought but she was still annoyed that Val had allowed herself to be charmed by Gary.

'You can tell them that I accept their offer. I'll talk to Val when she returns which should be any time now.'

Chapter 5

Ron was still feeling emotional following Libby's wedding. 'My little girl. I'm so glad that Carl was there to give her away. I know they're going to be happy, Claire but Val's going to be mad. I'm not sure she'll ever forgive her. And as for your mother...'

Claire wasn't entirely sure. 'If you'd said that to me a little while ago I would have agreed with you. But a woman I didn't know when I was alive has taken over my mother's mind and body so I'm never sure how she's going to react to anything these days.'

'Fair enough. Let's go and see Val and your mother and see how they're getting on.' Ron knew what Claire's answer would be but thought he'd try and get his own way for once.

'Sure, Ron.'

The surprise showed in his face, but not for long.

'After we've been to see how my father and Mel are getting on. This is going to amaze you, Ron.'

Knowing the amount of energy it took to argue with her when she was determined to have her own way, Ron decided to cede to Claire's wishes and prepared himself to be amazed.

*****

As it happened, he was amazed. 'Who the hell is that?' They were watching a man stretching in a gymnasium. Claire laughed as they looked around. Tony had given her the head's up about her father's new obsession. The gym was full of the usual torture equipment from treadmills, cross-trainers and all manner of weights, to complicated looking multi-gyms that Claire would never understand how to use or why anybody would want to. Her father had completed a number of stretches and looked as if he'd been running. He was a completely different man to the one that they had watched breakdown when his marriage and illicit relationship had imploded before his daughter had been kidnapped. Bulging with muscles and not an ounce of fat in sight, Claire was impressed with her father's transformation although he had gone completely over the top. He approached a bar with weights on each side that Claire thought would take ten men to lift. He lifted the heavy bar above his head with ease and Claire and Ron watched as additional weights were added. They weren't the only ones watching as other gym bunnies heard that Graham was in the building and stopped their workout to watch the locally famous strongman. He began to struggle as the pole became heavier and his muscles strained like those of the Incredible Hulk bursting out of his shirt. Satisfied with his workout, Graham eventually stopped and his audience applauded. He feigned embarrassment but was secretly delighted. He nodded in appreciation and saluted the crowd like a true champ. Claire cringed. Graham towelled the sweat from his face and the back of his neck while chatting to a few of his admirers about various techniques. When the crowd dissipated he took his mobile phone out of his rucksack and took it off do not disturb mode to check if he'd missed any calls. The *Eye of the Tiger* music rang out in the gym and Graham quickly answered the call. They listened to his side of the conversation as Graham said that he would come over for tea and would then take Mel to visit her friend Alice.

Ron tried to work it all out. 'First of all your father seems to have turned into Arnold Schwarzenegger and secondly, I think that was his ex Carol on the phone who last I heard didn't want anything to do with him?'

'Time's a great healer, Ron as you well know. Now come on.'

They followed Graham who arrived at Carol's house a little later. His daughter gave him a hug and a kiss as a normal greeting Claire noticed, and not as if they hadn't seen each other for a while. Graham pulled Carol into an embrace and kissed her on the cheek. Claire noticed the look between them and concluded that they were having a physical relationship.

'I wonder why they're hiding it?' asked Ron and Claire assumed it was for Melanie's sake.

'Perhaps they want to take it slowly until they're certain it's what they both want. Mel's had enough trauma and upset in her life and they'll want to protect her feelings.'

Ron couldn't imagine how he would have felt had Libby been kidnapped and put through the terror that Mel had encountered. She'd also had to come to terms with the fact that her father had another family and both parents had kept this from her for most of her young life.

'They seem to have forgiven your father and it all looks very cosy.'

They watched as the family sat together to eat their dinner with an amount of food on Graham's plate that Claire thought would feed a third world country for a week. Shortly after Graham and Mel said goodbye to Carol then left in Graham's car. They eventually pulled up outside a house, which Ron didn't recognise.

'You remember one of Mel's school friends? Well this is where the one called Alice lives.'

'One of the girls who was abused by Big Ed and his cronies?' Ron's voice turned to steel. The man had groomed the girls and arranged their deflowering as well as murdering his accomplice, and had escaped justice.

They watched as Alice's mother answered the door and let them in. Cups of tea were passed around amidst polite conversation and Alice used the excuse of wanting to show Mel some new clothes to get them away from the adults. She closed the bedroom door.

'So how are you really?'

'Still having nightmares and so is Drew, but the therapy's working for both of us and look.' Alice rolled up the sleeves of her blouse and presented her arms to her friend. Mel lifted them one by one and inspected both inside and out. There were some old scars, but nothing new.

'Well done, Alice. You're getting there.'

'It's not easy.'

Mel pulled her friend into a hug and both girls cried. She was so glad that Alice had stopped self-harming and hoped that she was on the road to a proper recovery.

They broke loose and dried their eyes. 'How about you?'

'I'm all right and the police think he's left the country now. Daddy's competition earnings means he can employ security staff as he likes to call them for when he's not with us, so at least that gives us peace of mind,' she sounded much older than her seventeen years to Ron and Claire, but that was expected after what she'd been through. 'But none of us will be able to move on properly until that evil bastard is caught and punished.'

'Hmm. I hope they castrate him.' Alice nodded.

'And men in prison have their wicked way with him,' said Mel and the girls giggled as they exchanged ideas for what would be the appropriate punishment for the man they knew as Big Ed.

When all ideas had been exhausted Mel resisted the urge to talk about Sandy's involvement in her escape. To her Sandy had been a heroine and she was still saddened at her violent death. But to Alice and

Drew she was a villain and almost as bad as Big Ed. They'd trusted her and she'd drugged them.

The conversation got onto safer ground and the girls talked about fashion and boys at Mel's dance class and Alice's badminton club. Graham called that it was time to leave and they hugged again and Mel left. Both girls felt better knowing that the other was on the mend.

Satisfied that her father and stepsister were as well as could be expected, Claire was ready to accompany Ron and to catch up with his wife and her mother.

*****

With the front seats extended well into the rear of the vehicle, Val and Gary tried to get some sleep. Val was both thirsty and uncomfortable and had only slept fitfully. Every time she'd managed to nod off a primal cry somewhere in the distance had shaken her fully awake and the last one had sounded too close for comfort. Gary had appeared to have been sleeping and had not jumped at the noise. However, he'd reached for his rifle, opened his eyes and the window and fired off a shot into the air. They'd heard some scurrying and all the other noises since then had been further away. Feeling slightly more relaxed but unable to sleep they'd started chatting. After she'd told him about her husband dying, Gary told her that his partner had died suddenly the previous year and that he'd been at a loss about what to do next. Val sensed that he didn't want to talk about her death so remained silent. Gary said he'd eventually decided to help those worse off than himself but still had to make a living. His company reduced their prices for charities and that way he earned enough to live on but was still able to do make a difference. Val felt a bond between them due to their shared experiences. She didn't know if it was their closeness in the vehicle, their intimate chat or the fact that they were at one with nature but their long kiss seemed like a natural progression. Gary's hand crept inside her top and Val realised that is was too soon for her. She pulled back.

'No, please stop.'

He withdrew his hand and as she opened her eyes, she thought she saw a flicker of frustration on his face, but put it down to the heat of the moment and her imagination.

'I'm sorry. I thought that was what you wanted?'

'No, I'm sorry,' she righted her clothes. 'I thought it was too, but it's too soon. I hope you understand?' she didn't want him to think she'd been leading him on.

'Of course, Val,' he took a hand and squeezed it reassuringly. 'You take as long as you like, this isn't a one night wonder.'

So he felt something too and he was willing to wait. Val was glad the Land Rover had broken down and they were stranded in the middle of nowhere. She wouldn't mention anything to Marion just yet as she hoped her friend would eventually come to like Gary, or at the very least, be happy for her.

They ate the last of the snacks as they watched the magnificent rise of the sun, and it wasn't much later that two of his staff turned up in another Land Rover to take them back to what passed for civilisation.

Ron and Claire watched as the vehicle approached the orphanage. The rescue vehicle had towed the Land Rover back. It was slow going and Val had opted to sit in the passenger seat while Gary steered the vehicle. They laughed and chatted during the journey and Val felt like she was at a party that she didn't want to end. She didn't notice the two police cars and Marion who appeared to be having an animated conversation with a uniformed officer. Gary did but chose to ignore it for the moment. He applied the handbrake and got out of the vehicle. He walked around to the passenger door, opened it and offered Val his hand. She accepted the gallant gesture even though she was perfectly capable of getting out of the Land Rover unaided. Gary pulled her into a hug and gave her a long, lingering kiss. Marion's conversation with the police sergeant stopped abruptly.

'I don't flaming believe it!'

'Madam?' said the sergeant relieved that the mad English woman had something else to focus her temper on.

Marion ignored him as she marched over to the Land Rover like a five year-old leaving a sweetie shop when told she can't have any goodies.

'What the hell?' seeing his wife being kissed so passionately was a total shock to Ron and he looked at Claire in confusion. She tried her best to keep her mouth shut and not to stare, completely agog at the scene before her. Something wasn't right. Not only was this public display totally out of character for Val, as soon as Claire had seen the man, alarm bells had started ringing and she knew that he was a bad one. Claire was surprised to see some evil souls hovering around him and knew that her and Ron would have to keep their guards up. There was something strangely familiar about the man and Claire scanned her memories but couldn't come up with a name. He certainly didn't look like anyone she'd encountered during her lifetime, but she was determined to find out more. Ron was too preoccupied for them to discuss the presence around the big man...

'Claire!'

'Sorry, sorry. I guess she's been able to move on,' oh Christ. Had she really said that out loud? 'What I mean...'

'I know exactly what you meant, Claire,' he folded his arms and she could see that it would take a lot of time and effort to make things right between them.

'I'm really sorry, Ron. That just slipped out. I didn't mean...' the words hung in the air and she forced herself to shut up before she did any further damage.

He unfolded his arms and stared at the scene below him, shaking his head. He looked distraught and she moved toward him and put an arm round his shoulder. Tears trickled down Ron's cheeks, slowly at first and then in a great torrent, accompanied by huge sobs.

'I miss her so much,' he stuttered between sobs and Claire hugged him, trying to hide her surprise. Because he'd considered moving to heaven for eternity no less, Claire had definitely not expected this reaction. She thought it best to keep quiet and she held him until the tears subsided.

'I'm going back, Claire. I don't want to watch any more.'

It was probably for the best and he did look absolutely drained. She gave him another squeeze. No words were needed.

'I'll see you when you get back,' and with that, he disappeared.

Val felt a sharp prod in the back of her shoulder as she broke from the kiss. If she had any doubts that it was Marion, the look of apprehension on Gary's face confirmed the fact. Val sighed. The magical moment had died and reality was back with a big thud. She turned around preparing to give it to her friend with both barrels.

'While you've been off gallivanting Mary's disappeared,' Marion's statement stopped Val in her tracks. Hands on hips and frowning, her friend looked as if she were about to explode.

'What do you mean disappeared?' asked Gary.

'I was talking to the organ grinder, not the monkey.'

'Marion! Please.' Val hissed. She would have words with Marion later about her rudeness to Gary but there were more urgent issues to deal with first. 'Just calm down and tell me what's happened.'

After the stress of the past 12 hours and little sleep the previous night due to the devastating news about Mary and worry about Val, Marion's nerves were in shreds. Having seen Val kiss *that man* as if they both hadn't a care in the world had tipped her over the edge, and she was now spoiling for a fight. Val's reasoned calm was enough to deflate her and any thoughts of further confrontation. Her shoulders literally dropped.

'Let's go in and you can update me on everything,' Val turned to Gary before walking away and he nodded in understanding.

'I'll go and see if Daniel needs any help.'

It was none of his business yet he was keen to help, thought Val as she walked to the orphanage with Marion. She'd tried to link her arm through Marion's to show support, but although obviously very upset, her stubborn friend had still shaken her off and it was taking an enormous amount of willpower for Val to remain calm and rational.

Claire was torn. Should she go back and support Ron, listen to what her mother and Val had to say, or follow the guy that Val had kissed? The unsettling feeling returned when she thought of the familiar stranger and that decided her next course of action.

Chapter 6

Ron and Sandy were on the settee in Cherussola. He hadn't meant to unburden to her but had been so upset.

'So how long has it been?' asked Sandy.

'One year, eleven months and three days,' he sighed. 'Of course I want her to move on but it was such a shock to see them kissing passionately, in broad daylight too!'

Sandy knew she couldn't say anything to make him feel better and he'd have to come to terms with his wife's new boyfriend. But she liked this kind, gentle man and wanted to be there for him. She took his hand and smiled and they sat like that for a while. Ron taking comfort from his new friend who had listened without making any judgements, and Sandy enjoying the company of a decent soul without fear of being thrown into any dark pits and subjected to never-ending pain and torture.

The double whoosh broke the spell and they let go of each other's hands to the amusement of Gabriella. She hid her smile as Raphael introduced himself to Sandy then got quickly down to business.

'We have reason to believe that the man who's seducing your wife is trafficking young girls.'

'Oh, not another one,' said Ron, remembering Big Ed. He forgot about Val for a moment as he recalled the circumstances of Sandy's passing.

'Are you okay?' he took her hand not concerning himself with what the angels would read into it. She nodded her head as Raphael continued.

'The vibes from the man are extremely bad and he has company,' seeing their confusion he elaborated. 'Evil souls are always with him. There's no doubt about where he'll go when his time comes, and he may even be groomed for advanced promotion down there.'

'So there's no hope for him at all?' said Sandy. Ron ignored her comment. 'And this is the man that my wife is seeing?' Ron was very frightened. 'We have to do something and damn quick.'

*****

Claire followed the man at a distance. The evil spirits accompanying him seemed too interested in his next move to bother with her, she wasn't even sure that they were aware of her presence. There was something in the way he carried himself that was familiar but she couldn't yet put her finger on it. Don't think of it and it'll come to you, she told herself as she watched him approach the office and close the door.

'All went to plan then?' Gary asked and Daniel nodded.

'You may have noticed the police presence,' he replied. 'Now isn't a particularly good time for this discussion.'

'Just chill and act like your normal self but show you're upset at the girl's disappearance. What do the police think?'

'That an animal's taken her. I told them I ran outside when I heard a scream and saw a lion carrying something in the distance, but that I couldn't make out what it was.'

'Did they believe you?' Gary wasn't overly bothered. It was handy having the Chief of Police as one of his clients and he knew he enjoyed young lithe girls much better than fully formed women. He also knew that as long as he kept him happy he needn't worry about being caught. Daniel needed to be kept on his toes though and there was no way he'd share the confidential information about his scumbag clients.

'There's no evidence to prove it or otherwise and they know we haven't had lions attack humans in this area for years,' he gave a sneaky smile and Gary knew there was more to come. 'That bloody woman Marion didn't believe it of course, until I told her that the reason she couldn't see the bodies of the other girls who'd disappeared was because we'd suspected lion attacks. She went ape and said that if we had warned everyone off, Mary would still be safe.'

'But you think she believed you?'

'Judging by her reaction, yes.' Marion had run to her room crying and when he'd sent the nurse to see her she'd been sobbing her heart out.

Daniel had done a good job and Gary gave him a manly pat on the back. 'Well done, mate. There may be a little bonus in this for you. We won't take anyone else from here until Marion and Val have gone and I'll arrange a hunting expedition and bring me back a rogue lion in the meantime.' It wouldn't do him any harm at all for Val to think he'd killed a lion that had a taste for human blood.

*****

Mary woke up in a comfortable bed wearing a strange nightdress and grabbed the wrist of the hand that was stroking her face. The girl who was looking down at her and smiling, jolted and tried to pull her hand away, to no avail. She saw the look of terror on the new girl's face and remembered how she'd felt on her first day.

'Please, I don't want to hurt you. I am your friend,' Tamara risked a little smile. 'They want me to tell you what you have to do if you want to eat and don't want to be beaten.'

Ten minutes later Mary sat with her knees hugged to her chest, arms folded around them with her head on her arms. She was absolutely terrified at what Tamara had told her and at first, hoped she was having a nightmare and would soon wake up. When the child realised that the nightmare was the reality of her existence, all hope disappeared and she sat on the bed sobbing her heart out. The memories of her family's murder came back to her, but before that she remembered the face of the group's leader who had raped her, and slapped her when she screamed with the pain. Her insides ached just thinking about it. She had scurried back to her family and now in her mind's eye she saw the picture of her mother being violated by a number of men. First by the one who had ruined her and then the others one at a time, while her father had been forced to watch. She could still hear the laughter of the others as they watched and Mary had had to bite her fingers until they bled, to stop herself from screaming out loud. They were all flung on top of each other like rubbish bags, after the men had finished, and bullets were fired as their attackers watched and laughed. And now, just when she thought she might have had a chance at a decent life, they wanted to turn her into an underage sex slave. Strange men would prod and poke her and she would have to perform for them and commit acts that she could never have imagined doing, until Tamara had slowly and calmly explained it all. And if she refused, they wouldn't feed her or allow her to sleep and she would die of starvation and exhaustion. There was one small consolation that if she kept secret would ruin their evil lives as much as they would ruin hers. She didn't dwell on that information because the personal consequences were too frightening. Mary's final thought before her body collapsed into a fatigued sleep, was that she must be a really evil child to be punished so much before she even had a chance of reaching adulthood.

*****

'Oh sweet Jesus,' Claire said out loud. She'd seen and heard enough and wanted to get back to safety to process the niggling thoughts in the back of her mind about this latest child abuser. The spirits that

57

hadn't appeared to notice her presence before turned away from their human and looked directly at her. Claire knew she was in trouble and hoped she'd be able to return to Cherussola before they caught up with her.

*****

Marion had been crying again but gave herself a good talking to about pulling herself together. Val was dying to know what had happened while she'd been out in the bush but remained calm and quiet until Marion was ready to explain. Seeing how upset she was, Val knew it must have been something awful and let Marion talk at her own pace, without interruption.

'A lion attacked and killed Mary and they think that's what happened to the other girls,' her hand covered her mouth as she thought of the awfulness of the situation. 'But how could? When...'

'When you were out sightseeing with your...' Marion looked down, refusing to make eye contact with Val, but the disgust showed on her face now that she'd regained her composure.

Val had had enough. 'I'll have you know that the Land Rover broke down,' she stood up and banged her fists on the chair arms, both women chose to ignore the clouds of dust that jumped from the chair and slowly floated back down. 'We would have been back much earlier and trust me, it wasn't fun out in the bush, wondering if we were going to survive until the morning.' That wasn't strictly true but Val wanted to make her point. She leaned toward her friend, her face inches away from Marion's. 'If you weren't so bloody jealous, maybe you'd have noticed that before this awful news, I was the happiest I'd been in ages.'

'Jealous! Jealous! Me?' For God's sake, Val, you can't seriously think...'

'This conversation is over, Marion. My focus now is to look after the children and ensure their safety. I thought we were meant to be friends but obviously...'

'Is now a bad time?' neither of them noticed that Gary had entered the room.

'No,' said Marion and Val shook her head. 'We need to build a barbed wire fence. Not sure how quickly we can get the wire but the sooner the better.'

'I'm already on it,' said Gary and Marion ignored the smug look from Val. 'Daniel's arranged for an armed guard for a few nights but the fence will be up by tomorrow night. My men will see to that.'

Val thanked him but Marion didn't acknowledge his comments, wondering why she was being made out to be the baddie of the piece.

'We need to get the children together and try to talk to them without terrifying them, though I'm not sure how we're going to do that.'

'Maybe I should come along and tell them about the guards and the guns?'

'That won't be necessary, Gary,' said Marion through gritted teeth. 'But thank you for arranging for the fence to be erected. You may want to get on with that now,' she dismissed him as if she were the head talking to a naughty pupil and he turned away to look out of the window for a moment, pretending to assess the area but calming himself until his eye stopped twitching. Perhaps Marion should have an encounter with a lion, he thought fleetingly before turning to Val. 'I'll catch up with you later.'

She leant over and kissed his cheek. 'Thanks, Gary.'

Marion wanted to vomit.

'Marion,' he said nodding and she nodded back in acknowledgement of his departure without saying a word.

*****

The angels and two spirits were discussing how best to warn Val about her evil suitor.

'I think Claire may want to tell her brothers then perhaps Tony can explain to Libby and she can speak to her mother on her return home?' said Gabriella. She could see that Raphael didn't know what she was talking about, so explained the siblings' ability to communicate with each other.

'She is special isn't she?' Gabriella noticed his tone of voice and was surprised. It had been a while since her twin had shown that sort of interest in anyone. Knowing that Claire had her faults but was intrinsically good and totally different to the last one, she was happy for him.

'Yeah, yeah, we all know how special she is.' Ron sounded petty even to himself, so tried to justify his words. 'What I meant to say is that can we stick to the point and try to find a way to warn Val off. I don't think they're due back for a while, Gabriella so we need something more urgent that your plan. Do you have any ideas, Raphael?... Raphael?'

'Claire!'

'What?' said Ron but Gabriella sensed a problem too. Not with the same foresight as her brother but she definitely felt the disturbance.

'Come on, before they get to her,' he turned to Gabriella. 'I'm not sure if Sandy's strong enough yet.'

The disturbance was getting stronger. 'We're going to need all the help we can get. Come on, I'll explain on the way.'

She was moving upwards as fast as she could but they were gaining on her. She'd looked back once and had been alarmed to see that the few evils had multiplied and the teenager who they'd encountered in the past had joined them. Had Claire had time to have a proper look she would have seen that he was stronger and now appeared to be in charge. She was terrified and images of the terrors that both Sandy and Ken had told her about passed before her eyes. Claire shook them away trying to concentrate all her efforts on moving upwards as fast as she could. She felt a gush of wind, caused by a hand swiping and missing her leg. She panted with the effort, knowing that this was a race she was unlikely to win and she felt the first hand make contact with her ankle. Trying to keep moving upwards with every fibre of her soul, her warped mind still had time to tell her that the calloused hand was covered in warts, and the second one had a finger missing. By the time the prodding hands were in double figures, she had stopped analysing their individual deformities. Only one set of hands had a body and face and when the teenager shoved his face directly into Claire's she screamed, wondering why on previous occasions, she hadn't noticed his likeness to Big Ed.

*****

Relations between Marion and Val were polite but frosty during the following days. They were both grieving over the loss of the girls and were able to use the grief to disguise what appeared to be the demise of their friendship. Val had been told about the early return to the UK and instead of the news of the new assignment bringing them closer, it had widened the gap. When Val had told Gary he had been distraught and the news of her departure had given their relationship a sense of urgency, which in turn made Marion even more distant. The fence was erected and despite Val's protests to the contrary, Marion was grateful for his help. She was annoyed that Val appeared to turn into an incapable useless female in Gary's presence, and wondered when she would swoon so her hero could pick her up and walk off with her into the sunset.

On the third day after Mary's disappearance before night turned to dawn, shots awoke the occupants of the orphanage. The children were told to remain in their accommodation and Val, Marion and Daniel almost collided at the bottom of the stairs. They heard another shot from the direction of the back of the building and walked cautiously toward the back door. Gary appeared with his uncocked shotgun over an arm and smiled reassuringly at the worried audience.

'One of the guards thought he saw something earlier tonight and the boss called me in,' he rubbed some sweat off his forehead. 'A large female's prowling the area. They say once they get a taste for human blood, they always come back for more.'

Val shivered and the others stared at him in horror.

'The only way to stop this is to kill her. I'm taking a party of men with me and we're going to hunt her down.'

Good grief! Marion thought as Val flung herself into Gary's arms telling him to be careful and to stay safe. She felt the need to do the right thing so wished him good luck and shook his hand. The feel of his flesh on hers gave her the creeps and it was a major effort to keep her expression impassive. The moment passed and she stepped back when Daniel stepped forward to shake his hand. Marion's bullshit-ometer almost went off the scale when she noticed the sly look that passed between the men. Something was afoot and she would do her utmost to find out what was really going on.

The hunting party were away the whole of that day and night and Val was almost beside herself with worry and retired to her room after dinner, saying that she wanted to be alone. Not that long ago she would have confided her fears in me, thought Marion sadly. Daniel had gone out for the night and Marion wondered if he were secretly meeting up somewhere with Gary. She took the time and opportunity to have a good look around the office, to see if she could find a reason for her suspicions and distrust of her co-worker. She flicked through the personal files of the children in the filing cabinet. At first she thought that all was in order but Mary's was missing, along with those of the other missing girls. She didn't know whether this was significant but planned to ask the police if they'd taken the files.

The desk drawer was easy to open with a bit of fiddling with a hairgrip. Marion had always thought it clichéd when she watched old-fashioned detective shows and they were able to pick locks with hair accessories, but it had actually worked! The papers weren't very well organised which told Marion that Enala, the very efficient and jolly administrator come part-time cleaner, did not have access to this drawer.

'Well, well,' she muttered to herself as she looked at two UK bank statements she'd found amongst the scribbled notes and other rubbish that was in the drawer. Why would Gary Jamieson pay Daniel Mulenga money into a UK bank account? As much as she pondered, Marion couldn't think of one legitimate reason. She also knew she'd have to figure this one out without the help of Val − when it came to Gary Jamieson, her friend's judgement could not be trusted.

*****

Mary didn't notice the fine quality of the transparent white negligee she wore as Tamara led her to the room where she was to be taught her trade. She was shaking nervously and wondered if she would be allowed to leave when they discovered she wasn't a virgin. She doubted it very much. It occurred to her that if she was no good, or if they discovered she wasn't pure, they would get rid of her rather than returning her to the orphanage. Mary wanted to survive to inflict as much damage as possible so put her fears to the back of her mind and hurriedly thought of the first part of her survival plan.

Claire tried her utmost not to panic as she fought with all her might. She knew it was a battle she couldn't win but was determined not to go down without a fight. She'd dispensed with some of them but that gave her scant satisfaction as for every hand that she was able to get rid of, at least another two had appeared in its place. The teenager seemed to be directing proceedings but didn't appear to be actively involved. Perhaps if she tried to get to him she'd scare off the weaker ones and have a better chance. He was very near to her face and smiling a triumphant smile. Claire thought for a moment that it was unlady-like but had been very effective when she'd seen it on a dramatisation once about one of the rougher places in England. She stopped struggling with the hands and returned his smile. He was confused for a second and she thrusted her head forward violently. The butt took him completely by surprise and he yelled and disappeared into the ether. Christ that hurt, thought Claire with satisfaction. She was still amazed that she could feel such horrendous physical pain even though she was dead. A few of the hands drifted away and she managed to gain some height. Her satisfaction soon disappeared when the teenager reappeared and ordered his minions to double their efforts. The hands multiplied and she was jolted as the direction changed and the journey downwards speeded up.

The teenager knew exactly who she was and recalled the occasion when he'd encountered her before and because of her strong guardians, had run away with his tail between his legs. He'd also heard the rumours about her talents and knew that the rewards for presenting his catch to his masters would be innumerable. But before that he wanted to get his own back and Claire had to suffer the indignity of the teenager's hands exploring regions that had not been explored since her final night with her fiancé, Jay. Her struggles were useless but she couldn't let him humiliate her without making an effort to stop him.

Gabriella took in the scene and wondered if they were too late, the evils were travelling quickly and the gates of Hell were in sight. The nearer they got the harder the task and the more likelihood of failure. She shook off the thoughts and concentrated on the job in hand. An idea was formulating and she turned to Raphael to give him instructions. He was way ahead and had separated from the rest, despite the risk to his own safety. Like a bolt of lighting he crashed through the atmosphere, determined to cause as much chaos as possible and to save the damsel in distress.

The shock of the violence had initially forestalled her aggressors but had eventually strengthened them. Claire remembered the love circle she had shared with Raphael and Ron and despite the pain and discomfort, squeezed her eyes shut and tried to focus on only good memories of love and happiness. She felt a whoosh and a lessening of hands and tried to push down the smugness brought on by a faint hope that her plan was actually starting to work. Claire had a sensation of hovering between two worlds and realised that this must have been what both Sandy and Ken before her felt when rescued by Gabriella. The penny still hadn't dropped and she decided to risk a peep, opening one eye slowly and scanning the area. The white clothed black angel whooshed past her, lighting up the dark atmosphere as he did so. Claire's mouth hung open as Raphael's head made contact with the teenager she now thought of as Big Ed's son. Both angel and demon disappeared into the atmosphere and knowing for definite that there was hope, Claire doubled her efforts, thinking only pleasant, loving thoughts. Gentle hands groped and found hers and she was now part of a circle of goodness with Gabriella, Ron and Sandy. Sandy had been terrified of returning towards hell but had fought the demons in her memory and had bravely accepted the challenge.

They made slow and steady progress and all except Gabriella started to relax. They realised their mistake when a roar of biblical proportions shook their circle and the air around them. Looking down they saw a regiment of demons and their animal slaves heading purposefully and determinedly upwards towards them.

'Concentrate!' screamed Gabriella as she led the circle upwards towards safety as fast as she could. She tried to hide her fear but Claire sensed it straight away and it wasn't long before Ron and Sandy picked up on their emotions.

'Oh, no,' Sandy wailed and was inconsolable.

Gabriella would meet the worst fate – it had been centuries since the evils had captured their last high-level angel Zach, and he was kept down there, not giving them the opportunity to rescue him. As far as Gabriella knew he might be tortured on a daily basis or even be a slave of the evils. What she did know for definite was that he hadn't turned to the evil side.

She shuddered as she saw the enemy gaining on them.

Salvation arrived in a timely fashion. As the evils neared, the whoosh of light returned and like a rocket, Raphael hit them from below and propelled the circle upwards. They gained strength as the distance between them and their evil enemy grew and they were able to slow down and watch the demons fall back to hell as if being pushed off invisible ladders. They were too shaken to appreciate the punishment that the demons would receive having been so near to, but now lost their great prize.

Claire was shaking as she threw herself into Raphael's body. The impact winded him but he recovered enough to hold her, his soothing words caressing like hot chocolate on a cold winter's night.

'I thought they had me,' she gulped. 'I thought that was it... for eternity,' she broke away, embarrassed at the lack of control over her emotions. 'Thank you, Raphael, I will never forget this as long as... well, for all eternity.' She was almost back to her old self and turned when she heard Ron cough.

'Thank you too, Ron, Gabriella and Sandy. It was so brave of you all, especially you, Sandy... I...' she'd lost control again and Raphael pulled her into a hug. Facing the others with Claire's head hidden in his shoulder he loosened one arm from around her back and shooed them away with his hand.

Back in Cherussola, Gabriella settled Ron and Sandy on the settee and told them to expect a debriefing when Raphael and Claire returned. She left them there to comfort each other and disappeared. The episode had shaken Gabriella more than she cared to admit and she wanted to talk to her brother and Claire before going off to lick her wounds in private. She found them shortly after, arms around each other. Before it became too embarrassing to watch, Gabriella gave a gentle cough to make them aware of her presence.

Totally absorbed with each other, they jumped when they heard the noise.

'Sorry to disturb you but we need to talk...'

'I was just comforting Claire. You can see how upset she is.'

So that's what they called it. 'I can see that. But before you get too err... comfortable, we need to explain some things to Claire if she's going to have a bigger role in our fight against evil.'

That was news to Claire and there was no way she wanted to encounter the evil spirits any time soon. Their sheer number had surprised her, and she had convinced herself that they would prevail and eventually their evil would overcome any good that Gabriella, Raphael and the other good spirits could muster.

Gabriella explained that her fear was a normal and expected reaction after what she'd just experienced.

'Not all are servants of the demons. That would cause chaos and an unnatural balance against us. We have containment centres.'

Gabriella waited for the questions and was impressed that Claire managed to keep quiet for a few minutes. Raphael could see it was a battle of wills between the two women but knew that Claire didn't stand a chance against his sister, yet.

'Where are these centres?' Claire couldn't help herself.

'We can't contain them here, there are far too many of them. You will have heard of the expression *hell on earth*?' Claire inclined her head. 'Well this is one of the places…'

Having almost experienced the real hell, Claire had no desire to see the earthly version. She had heard many people exaggerate and refer to it, but never in a million years had she thought the place existed, literally. If this was part of her learning experience or to do with her so called *special* talents she could very well do without it. She closed her eyes and tried to inject some brave serum into her thoughts but her experience of the probing hands had affected her more than she cared to admit. Despite Claire's natural curiosity and almost manic desire to know what was going on in the universe, she really did not want to go.

Seeing the expression on Claire's face didn't need a mind reader to know what she was thinking. Raphael knew that she had to meet some tough challenges and he'd already argued with Gabriella about what was and was not appropriate. His need to keep her out of harm's way clashed with her training requirements. Although he accepted that she had to face some fears to enable her to reach her full potential, he just wanted to love and protect her and was sure that there would be further disagreements with both his sister and mother about the best way forward. Gabriella hadn't flexed her wings and looking at his sister there was no tension or the look of concentration on her face that signalled imminent action. Even their mother couldn't recognise the barely perceptible twinkle in her eyes that showed her twin she wanted to have a bit of fun. Had it been with anyone else Raphael might have joined in, but he hated seeing his Claire looking so vulnerable and terrified. Casting a glance at Gabriella and shaking his head he put an arm around Claire. Wrapped in the warmth and safety of her new love she closed her eyes, hoping to garner strength from him. Her trembling stopped.

He pushed a few curls behind her ear and put his lips to it. 'You don't have to go there, just watch. You need to know about this but must not discuss it. Understand?'

Claire felt like a pupil again and she relaxed against him while the scene below unfolded.

A group of explorers were walking through a forest. One looked up but the canopy of trees blocked out the light and he wiped the sweat from his forehead. It was a fruitless exercise as within seconds, his head was wet again. His shirt was stuck to his body and he sighed and carried on walking, determined to find the cave that the indigenous people had written about for centuries but had to date remained illusive. The humidity was draining and the group plodded on slowly until they came into the clearing. Pressing on he told the others to follow him down into the bottom of the valley where he was almost sure lay the entrance to the cave. He looked up at the sheer cliff face and risked a glance skyward. The forecast had been for dry, sticky weather and it wasn't even the wet season so he was surprised to see the dark clouds slowly gathering. Men had already died trying to find this place and Chris weighed up his options. Wiry and fit but at 72 he knew he didn't have many chances left and had agreed with his wife that this would be his final attempt at this particular quest. He studied his son who was laughing and joking with the others, the centre of attention as usual. Ralph was a lover of adventure but with a low boredom threshold and Chris knew his son didn't have the interest or determination to carry this through to the end after he retired. He closed his eyes and sighed, it was his dream and not Ralph's and he couldn't expect to live the rest of his life through his son. Ignoring the clouds but with a sense of foreboding he ordered the group to move on. As in previous expeditions this was where the locals left them. The tales of the place that had been instilled in them since childhood were still fresh in their memories and none would go willingly into *infierno terrenal*.

Halfway down Ralph called to his father. 'Take a look at the sky!'

Chris didn't need to look. He threw his pickaxe into the cliff wall in frustration and leaned into it, his head resting on his forearm while he tried to control his emotions. He'd willingly risk his own life to be able to realise his lifelong dream of finding the legendary cave that others doubted existed. He'd been ridiculed and laughed at and his many other discoveries had been negated by stubbornness and sheer refusal to admit that the cave known to the locals as *hell on earth* was purely a myth. If they pressed on and any of the group were swept away in the downpour, could he live with that on his conscience? He looked at them one by one, each seeing the question in his eyes and the answer was the same from all five, a definite shake of each head. As his son moved across the rock face and put a hand on his father's arm, Chris felt no comfort from it, knowing that his efforts had been thwarted once again.

'Will you tell him when his time comes?' asked Claire, more to herself than to the angels. There was something else going on in the scene that she was trying to put her finger on but couldn't quite figure it out.

'That's it,' she snapped her thumb and middle finger together. 'I've got it. Ralph is one of ours isn't he?'

Raphael's feeling of pride hid his initial shock. Claire was full of surprises and Gabriella might have been able to hide her own shock from Claire, but he could see right through her.

'What makes you think that, Claire?'

'I honestly don't know, Gabriella. I just know he's an old soul and a good one. I saw a kind of light shining around him, it was coming and going though. Does that make any sense?'

They could see she was trying to figure it all out and knew there was no point in doing so. Claire's talents were a natural gift and the longer she remained in Cherussola, the stronger her gift would become. Neither had seen a gift develop so quickly and Gabriella wondered whether it was all actually Committee given or related to her ancestry. Raphael was deep in thought too, probably wondering the same thing, assumed Gabriella.

'You are absolutely right, Claire,' she decided not to tell her that it could take centuries for some to see what Claire had been able to in such a short time. 'Let's watch the rest and we'll talk again later.'

Gabriella's comments lacked the usual impatience and Claire sensed a new level of respect toward her. Something was going on here but she decided not to push it and for once, remained silent.

'Just watch,' whispered Raphael putting an arm around her waist and pulling her closer to him as the rain took hold and the men in the scene below made their way back up the cliff as fast and as carefully as their weary legs could take them. Claire assumed correctly that Ralph had arranged the rain as a timely deterrent.

The scene changed and it seemed like a different day. The rain had stopped and the explorers were nowhere to be seen. The plants and vegetation were thick and heavy in the area on display and even if the valley hadn't been flooded, Claire thought there was little or no chance of anyone finding the entrance to the cave. Eventually they were shown the covered entrance and taken inside the dark cave. Claire could see the narrow passages and wet walls that appeared to go on forever, downwards and downwards. Even the most intrepid and talented explorer would find it difficult to survive in this place, never mind overcome it. When she was starting to get bored by the never-ending maze of passageways, one opened out into a large area with a pond at one side. She assumed that this was sometimes drier or bigger depending on the level of rainfall, the season, or whether there had been heavenly intervention.

'What's moving?' she leaned over, trying to get a better look at the high ceiling of the cave, which appeared to be moving of its own volition. Once her eyes adjusted to the dimmer light, she saw small wings upon wings coming and going and realised that the cave was teeming with bats.

'Yuck.'

On further inspection, Claire could also see that the floor appeared to be moving and when she identified the presence as cockroaches, she was even more disgusted. Gabriella and Raphael or their assistants viewed the cave on a regular basis, so what came as a surprise to Claire was no more than routine to them. They spent the time watching her reactions and both knew that Claire wasn't going to figure it out.

'It does look like Hell on Earth, but there's obviously something I'm not getting here?' she looked to Gabriella for guidance.

'The bats are good souls...' said Raphael.

'...and the cockroaches are evils...' this from Gabriella and it reminded Claire of her brothers doing their twin conversation tag. Silence followed until she shook herself back to attention.

'...We catch them and deposit them in the cave for eternity. They live on the guano produced by the bats.'

Claire looked from one to the other, wondering how angels were selected for the bat jobs.

'We have a rota for the bats, and most of us have had a stint,' said Gabriella. 'Trust me, it's not that bad unless...oh no,' she tensed. 'I'll be back shortly. Raphael explain please.' She disappeared with the usual whoosh and Raphael told Claire to keep watching.

After sleeping all day, the bats flew toward the cave's entrance. 'They feed mainly on mosquitos,' said Raphael. 'Keeping that population down is important to alleviate even more human suffering.

As the bats neared the cave entrance Claire saw something move in the undergrowth. The giant slithering object raised itself to its full size and struck. The first bat to leave the cave was taken completely by surprise as the boa seized its prey in its jaws and wrapped several coils around its victim, constricting until the bat had suffocated. The snake swallowed the bat headfirst. Claire knew this was no ordinary snake when she saw it kill and swallow another two bats in quick succession.

'I thought they had to digest their prey first and wouldn't need to eat anything else for a while?' she'd remembered something from the nature programmes she'd been encouraged to watch as a child.

'The only snakes that can find their way to the cave are those evils put there by the demons. They create as much havoc as they can and we have to sort it before it gets out of hand. Gabriella has taken a team to save the souls of the bats, but watch.'

A man holding a large knife appeared behind the snake. Claire thought it strange that the snake hadn't detected his arrival by tremors on the ground and on closer inspection, noticed that the man was Ralph, the one she'd seen the light around earlier.

By the time the snake sensed the movement behind him it was too late and the knife had chopped off his head. The rest of his body slithered, taking a few seconds before messages from the reptile's brain stopped and the snake was eventually completely still. Taking no chances the man calmly and efficiently chopped the snake into small pieces. Once satisfied that he'd completed his gruesome task, he wiped the knife on some large leaves nearby, returned it to its sheath, and disappeared back into the undergrowth.

'So what happens if the bats are overcome by snakes and they kill a lot of them? Do the roaches escape and look elsewhere for food?'

'Claire,' Raphael's eyes bored into hers and all trace of fun and warmth had disappeared. 'When the demons have many evils to do their bidding, war, disease and pestilence are rife.'

'Has it ever happened?'

Raphael laughed without humour. 'Look back in history for an answer to that.'

Although safe and warm in his arms, a shiver ran through Claire. She knew she was being educated and trained for a purpose but hoped she'd never have to experience another evil encounter without Raphael by her side.

'How does it work with the angels on Earth?' Raphael replied with a kiss and she put her natural curiosity aside to deal with a more immediate need.

Both the first encounter with evils and the latest one to save the souls of the angel bats had left Gabriella feeling drained. She took no comfort from the familiar surroundings of her own wonderful white world. Dealing with evils made her feel unclean both mentally and physically and she vomited until there was nothing left. She then washed in pure water until all traces of evil had been completely purged from her system. Feeling more like her angelic self, she went to rally her troops and to find Ron and Sandy. Looking back to the first encounter Gabriella knew the reason the man was being shadowed by so many evils, what she didn't know was who he was.

*****

As much as Mary cleaned her teeth and rinsed her mouth, she couldn't get rid of the foul taste of the man she'd had to pleasure. Besides for this she was pleased he'd believed her about her monthlies and that she'd been able to set the date that she was supposed to lose her virginity, almost a week later. She was quickly learning that they thought with their snakes and not their brains and she would use this to her advantage. Before her *big day* the following week, he wanted to teach her a number of other tricks and she would have to spend the time in between her lessons planning how to deceive her trainer into thinking she was a virgin.

75

The lion hunters returned triumphant early the following morning, with a lion that caused awe and amazement amongst all the orphans and staff, and wonder in the villages both near and far afield. Marion nearly vomited when she saw Val practically throw herself at Gary, telling him how brave and fearless he was. Now that she knew that something was going on with Gary and Daniel, Marion noticed the conspiratorial looks between them and wondered how she and Val had missed them in the past.

So Gary and his team of hunters were hailed as heroes and the orphanage population were able to sleep easy that night for the first time since Mary's disappearance.

Looking at Gary made Val realise how much she cared for him. Not only was he lovely to look at, thoughtful, caring and incredibly macho, he had also risked his own life to save children who hadn't had a very good start in theirs. Val was certain she could trust him; the only downside to their relationship was the falling out with Marion. She hoped that they could get over that hurdle and be friends again, sooner rather than later. When the adoration had died down, Val leaned up and whispered in Gary's ear. A lecherous smile spread across his face and he looked down at Val and nodded, kissing her cheek at the same time. The look wasn't lost on Marion and she guessed what was planned for later that night. When for a moment she locked eyes with Val, she gave a tiny shake of her head. Val shook her own head slowly then gave Gary a long kiss on the lips, answering Marion's silent question. Marion left the foyer without a single word and made her way upstairs to her bed. She knew without doubt that she'd have to deal with the fallout from Val's doomed relationship; the only question mark was when that would be.

The man had insisted she perform the disgusting act. Luckily he'd drank a lot as she'd hoped, and hadn't noticed her trying not to gag as his eyes had been closed for most of the time. Mary made a mental note. She'd have to learn to overcome the disgust and please them so they'd keep coming back. She'd managed to sneak the stuff into his drink as Tamara had instructed. Even with the drink and the drug he had still had full sex with her, although she was sure he wouldn't be able to remember much about it. He was now sleeping and she'd smeared the blood she'd hidden earlier onto the bed sheet. When he awoke he would naturally assume that he'd taken her virginity. Mary could then relax and bide her time knowing that for every one that forced themselves upon her, the legacy would be a ticking time bomb of disease that they might be able to control but could never diffuse.

*****

'Where are they?' Gabriella was surprised that Raphael and Claire hadn't yet returned to the common room.

'If you mean Claire and Superman,' said Ron, 'don't know. I haven't seen Claire so shaken before so I assume she's still resting.'

Resting was probably the wrong word thought Gabriella but decided to leave them to it. 'We need to go and find out more about the man being shadowed by the evils,' she saw the look of terror on Sandy's face. 'Don't worry, we're taking plenty of back-up with us this time.'

'But, Gabriella, what if...'

'You'll be perfectly safe, Sandy. This time. Sometimes we all have to do things outside our comfort zone. It makes us stronger.'

Ron nearly choked. Maybe running a marathon or climbing a mountain was his idea of doing

77

something outside his comfort zone, not battling with evil, deranged souls whose sole purpose was to take pleasure from inflicting maximum pain for eternity.

'Ron?'

'Ready when you are, Gabriella,' it wouldn't do Sandy any good to see that he was bricking it as much as she was.

*****

Claire must have fallen asleep. Despite her near hell experience and the revelations that followed it, she woke up feeling completely happy and safe. Opening her eyes she took in her surroundings. Everything was a brilliant white and seemed to ooze sparkle, but without dazzling. The bed was the most comfortable she'd ever laid on and she felt as if she were being softly caressed, without actually being touched. The walls appeared to be covered in soft, large white feathers and when she got up from the bed and ran her hand down the wall, she giggled at the softness beneath her fingers.

'You're awake then?'

She turned to see her hero and they smiled at each other. Raphael opened his arms and it was the most natural thing for Claire to enter his embrace. She looked up at him and he leaned down. Their lips touched and Claire thought she would explode with light. She didn't want that kiss to end but Raphael wanted to be absolutely sure this was the right time. He knew she was vulnerable because of the attack and still stunned having seen hell on earth, but wanted her to be with him because she found him attractive, not because she was in awe of him.

He leaned back and looked down at the lovely spirit in front of him. He loved the springiness of her dark, curly hair. Revelling in the touch of it he didn't stop as he looked into her beautiful deep grey eyes.

'Are you absolutely sure, Claire that this is what you want?'

'I've never been so sure of anything,' was he completely stupid?

Raphael took off his robe and she gasped. Perfectly toned and such a touchable chest. She ran her fingers along his shoulders, chest and down to his boxers, delighting in the silkiness of the hard muscles. Before she could explore further, he stepped back and flexed his wings.

'Show off.' Claire laughed and he was enchanted, sweeping her off her feet he carried her to the bed like a knight who'd won his princess.

Much later when Claire had been dazzled by love and brightness and, if she were totally honest with herself, a hefty dose of lust, she forgot about earlier events. She was convinced that she had already reached heaven and didn't need any other version of eternity.

*****

Chapter 7

When she looked down at the scene unfolding below them and recognised the man, despite the changes, Sandy thought it was some sort of sick joke or test. Ron noticed her distress as she paled considerably.

'How could you?' she covered her mouth with a hand and shook her head.

Gabriella was as baffled as Ron. Sandy saw the confused looks on their faces and began to wonder if they actually did know who he was. She tried to compose herself but her voice still shook, such was the impact of seeing the man who'd tormented her in life before ending her earthly existence.

'You really don't know?'

It was obvious they hadn't a clue and now it was Sandy's turn to be confused. She addressed Gabriella. 'But I thought you had special powers and knew everything?'

'We do our best, Sandy. Feel free to share when you're ready,' Gabriella couldn't hide her impatience and didn't like the fact that Sandy had information that she had somehow missed. Her sarcasm was lost on Sandy who was still upset.

'That's Big Ed!' it was almost a whisper but the words could have been screamed, such was their impact on Ron. He reeled with the information and his initial response was denial. He held back, admitting deep down that Sandy must know for certain as her physical reaction left no room for doubt.

So he'd changed his appearance and was pimping his evil trade elsewhere thought Gabriella as she pondered the company that was shadowing him without his knowledge.

'We have to stop him,' Gabriella heard the panic in Ron's voice as they watched his wife as she flirted with the man in the Land Rover, and they wondered where he was taking her. It was pretty obvious to anyone who observed the scene that they were close but Ron hoped they weren't that close.

*****

'Where are we staying?'

'It's a surprise, beautiful lady. You just sit back and enjoy the ride,' he patted Val's thigh and somewhere way up above them her former husband shuddered, trying to quell the panic that was slowly threatening to overcome him.

She was surprised she'd fallen asleep and the jolt of the vehicle shook her awake.

'Sorry, Val, but we're here.'

He watched her stretch and was looking forward to exploring her delicious womanly body later on. Gary was experiencing feelings for this woman that he hadn't had in years and the anticipation was making him nervous.

Val looked at the breath taking surroundings. There were a number of chalet type buildings set within what appeared to be a tropical garden. There was a curvy but wide snake- shaped swimming pool which a few swallows were flying around and occasionally dipping into. Three zebras were grazing on the grass in the distance and Val stood mesmerised while Gary took their bags out of the Rover and waited patiently. When she felt his eyes boring into her she shook herself out of her daydream.

'Sorry.'

'No need, Val. Most people have the same reaction,' he realised his faux pas. 'It's only business associates I've brought here, I didn't mean...'

It was the first time she'd seen him flustered. 'It's okay. You don't have to explain.'

'But I want you to know that this is special,' he put down the bags and took both her hands in his, speaking earnestly. 'Honestly, Val, I really don't want

81

you to think I make a habit of this.' Gary wasn't sure how to handle his feelings, but knew it was important for her to believe him. He was relieved when she reached up and kissed him.

'I believe you. Now shall we go and check in?'

Ten minutes later they were in the chalet, both nervous and for the first time, feeling awkward around each other.

'We're supposed to be adults,' said Val. 'This is bloody ridiculous.'

'Are you hungry?'

Val agreed that dinner was a great idea and hoped that they'd relax enough to be able to make full use of the lovely room later.

They were back to their usual selves at dinner and enjoyed each other's company. The steak was delicious and the wine flowed and they stopped on the way back to the chalet to look at the beautiful night sky. Val never ceased to be amazed by the lack of light pollution and the regular appearance of shooting stars. The one tonight reminded her of her late husband and she wished she hadn't thought of him while she was hoping to start a physical relationship with Gary. He sensed the change in her mood and assumed it was due to a small gust of wind.

'Shall we go inside?' not waiting for an answer, Gary unlocked the door and pushed it open, holding it so she could enter first. Val smiled at her perfect gentleman and didn't comment as he brushed up against her as they went inside. They fell onto the bed silently and started to undress. The night sky, the surroundings and their want of each other had all fuelled their passion and the kissing and touching became more urgent. Val knelt backwards and raised her arms for Gary to pull off her top. He lifted it and nuzzled his head in her breasts, enjoying the feel of a fully rounded woman.

'Gabriella,' pleaded Ron. 'Do something!'

The lightning lit up the whole room like a stark operating theatre and Val almost jumped off the bed when it was closely followed by the loudest clap of thunder she'd ever heard.

'Jesus!' she shouted and the mood was instantly broken. Val couldn't recapture her earlier feelings and she couldn't stop thinking about Ron. They tried to rekindle the passion but she felt awful and explained to Gary that she was sorry, but the time just wasn't right. She was relieved when he stroked her face and said that he understood, but he was a red-blooded male and she knew that if she couldn't give him what he needed, he would find it elsewhere.

'Thank you.' Ron was relieved and grateful for the lovely angel's intervention. He knew they could sometimes change weather patterns but generally only did so to save a large number of lives, or so he'd been informed.

Gabriella smiled angelically before giving the order for her host of angels to standby. She fully expected another onslaught from the evils, but this time she was ready for them. It didn't transpire. The teenager who Claire had thought of as Big Ed's son had carried out a silent appreciation of the situation. His previous punishments had made him wary and he wasn't prepared to start another battle that he couldn't win.

Gabriella harrumphed at the cowardice of the evils and gave the order to return to Cherussola. This was a battle she was sure she would fight another day.

*****

Marion heard the Land Rover pull up outside the orphanage the following morning and had a sneaky look out of her window. She saw Val lean in and give him a quick peck on the cheek. Marion would have expected something more lingering after their supposedly big night of passion and she wondered what had happened. Maybe that was just wishful thinking on her part, she sighed and turned away from the window to make her way downstairs. Marion hoped that when they left the following week, the distance between Val and Gary would cool their relationship but knowing Val as she did, she very much doubted it. Whatever happened between those two, she knew that if she wanted to work with Val in Romania they'd have to try and bury the hatchet that Gary had used, in her opinion, to break up their once unbreakable friendship.

Gary waved to Val after he dropped her off at the orphanage then watched in his rear-view mirror as she disappeared inside. They'd had a great night and he'd never shared as many of his inner feelings and hopes for the future with anyone like he had with Val. It had seemed completely natural and he knew it was too late to be careful because he'd fallen hook, line and sinker. There was no way she'd make him hurt her like Sandy and the ones before her had. Val was completely different and he'd cherish her. Despite or because of these emotions, Gary was frustrated and as horny as hell. The more he thought of Val the more he needed to dip his wick and the easiest way to do so would be with one of the youngsters. It wasn't as if he was being unfaithful to Val if he went with a youngster – his warped brain convinced him. He'd heard good things about the new girl so phoned his manager to tell him to make sure she was ready by the time he arrived.

*****

Gabriella, Ron and Sandy had returned to the sofa at Cherussola and found Claire and Raphael waiting for them. When they explained what had happened, the jigsaw pieces in Claire's mind started to fit together but she still had lots of questions.

'So you reckon Big Ed has had some sort of surgery to change his appearance and he's trying it on with Val?'

'But how could that happen and where's my mother? Are you okay, Ron? Of course you're not, that was a stupid question. And what about you, Sandy? It must have been awful when you realised and terrifying. And how did you find out it was...'

'QUIET!' Gabriella knew that shouting was the only way to stop Claire's stream of questions and Claire shut-up, mid flow.

Raphael squeezed Claire's hand and winked at his twin. Gabriella tried to ignore him and remain serious for a few minutes.

'Firstly, we don't know how that happened but assume that your mother was still at the orphanage while they stayed overnight in a hotel. Ron was deeply shocked but is okay now. It was awful for Sandy and she was terrified. And lastly, Sandy recognised Big Ed despite the fact that he must have had extensive facial surgery for no-one to realise before.'

'Err, did they... um. I mean are they...'

Claire was about as subtle as a ton of bricks thought Ron. 'Gabriella arranged a diversion in the form of a freak storm which cooled their ardour considerably.'

'Gabriella,' said Raphael, chastising more like a father than a brother. 'What will mother say?'

The others realised that there were limits to what the angels should do, but this was the first time that it had been discussed in front of them. It was also the first time that they had seen anyone question Gabriella's authority and they were fascinated by the interaction.

'I won't tell if you don't,' she responded.

'It was my fault, Gabriella and I'll take any punishment that your mother deems appropriate.'

The other spirits watched as Gabriella and Raphael laughed hysterically at Ron's comments. They had no idea why it was so funny but it wasn't long before they joined in, the tension and worry of recent events receding like a puddle evaporating in the desert.

The laughter eventually subsided and Ron remembered that there was a fair chance that his wife would sleep with the man who had arranged the kidnap of Claire's stepsister, who had groomed and ruined a number of other girls, and who had abused and murdered the lovely lady sitting next to him on the sofa. He explained his worries and the group turned serious again.

'The good thing for you, Ron is that he's going to die and that may happen before there are any further developments in his relationship with Val.'

Ron was grateful for Gabriella's choice of words.

'We all die, Gabriella, eventually,' said Claire.

'What my sister means, princess, is that Big Ed will die before he's old,' he kissed her to stop any further questions and the others stared as if witnessing a motorway pile up. 'And we know this because of the number of evil spirits travelling with him. His time is not quite up, but it won't be too much longer.'

'He's already been claimed by the master of evil and we're going to have to double our defences when that one arrives. He's big trouble,' Gabriella added, almost to herself.

Despite the thought of more trouble, Ron hoped that Big Ed's death would happen before he had a chance to leave his mark on Val.

'His son seems to be with him all the time. Do you think his time is close?' Claire hoped so for everybody's sake, especially Ron's.

'Not necessarily, Claire,' Gabriella frowned. 'Those with great evil often attract the demon mischief makers and that isn't his son by the way, it's his father.'

Gabriella explained that the teenager had seduced Big Ed's mother. He'd become bored when the baby was less than a year old and had murdered the baby's mother one night after an argument. He'd died the same night in a gang fight and the child had been brought up by elderly grandparents who had died when he was fifteen. Already out of control by that age he'd become a ward of court and was put into a home. He kept running away and when he turned sixteen the authorities stopped bringing him back. He had a tough time on the streets at first but the leader of a local gang took him under his wing and the rest is pretty obvious.

Despite his sorry start in life, none of them had any sympathy for Big Ed.

'What happened to his mother?' Sandy asked. Curious to know whether she might meet her at some stage.

'Back on Earth and living a good life,' Gabriella smiled. 'She's going to come to us eventually. She's already proved her worth so she just has to carry on along the same path. But never mind about her,' she rubbed her hands together as if she had a treat. 'Watch this...'

The scene below showed a family laughing and joking in their Mediterranean garden having just finished their evening meal. The sun was slowly disappearing in the pinky orange sky and the focus moved from the family onto a small puddle of water at the bottom of the garden. The insect sniffed the air detecting the presence of carbon dioxide and lifted itself from the puddle, its wings beating between 300 to 600 times per second to facilitate the move.

Harry looked at herself in disgust. A mosquito and a female to boot. Would her torture never end? Stupid question she said to herself knowing the answer was that it wouldn't. That's why she, he revised his thoughts – no, he maybe a she this time, but he was definitely a he – that's why he wanted his son to die as soon as possible. He could sense his strength and hoped that his own standing would improve with the arrival of his son. He had done his best and almost brought not one, but two senior angels to the demons, plus the one they were training and who didn't yet know how powerful she was. And what had he got in return? Punished for failure, that's what. They hadn't even acknowledged how close he'd come and all those who were with him were also punished so they'd resent him for a very long time. He'd have to watch his back when he returned but until then he needed to eat, never mind how disgusted he felt about it.

By the time the family heard the buzzing it was too late and the little girl was scratching her arm. Harry was long gone. Despite himself he'd enjoyed the taste of that blood and regardless of the danger, would try and feed off that young girl again. He flew around trying to find a suitable location to lay eggs and to populate the world with more of the deadliest animals on Earth.

'So there's no hope for him and others like him?'

'That's right Ron,' it was Raphael who answered and he scratched his chin.

'Not quite true,' said Gabriella and Ron, Sandy and Claire looked at the angels in confusion. Raphael inclined his head, indicating that Gabriella should explain.

'The ones who are pure evil have no desire to leave and simply want to climb the ladder to become a torturer rather than a victim. The weak ones will do exactly what they are told in the hope that they will eventually move higher up the chain and therefore suffer less,' she smiled at Sandy. 'And I think you know what happens to the lucky ones who take their torture but refuse to be bent to the ways of eternal evil. These souls will overcome and eventually we will rescue them.'

'How long does it take to rescue them, on average?' asked Claire.

'So many questions, Claire. You are intrinsically curious.'

Ron could see Claire's confusion. 'Nosey. Gabriella's saying you're nosey.'

'I like to learn,' she said. 'So how long then?'

'We do our best, Claire but we have many issues to deal with and have to prioritise,' Raphael gave her a squeeze. 'But the good ones are rescued eventually and each life is looked at by the Committee and their future decided.'

'What if both you and the demons want to claim a soul?' it was Ron this time.

'I'd love to say that good always conquers but that's just not true,' Gabriella sighed. 'We always get the good ones but sometimes mistakes are made and they have a stint down there before coming to us. It doesn't happen very often though.'

Ron and Sandy were quiet and for once Claire didn't ask any further questions. Poor Sandy had already suffered in hell but that had been the Committee's decision. With so many souls leaving the living plain the day that Claire and Ron had died, they were both extremely relieved that there hadn't been a mix-up and that they'd ended up in the right place. The consequences of a mistake of that magnitude were too horrendous to imagine. Claire was beginning to realise why it was wise for those in the land of the living to know very little about life in the hereafter.

Chapter 8

Although she'd done everything she'd been taught and tried her very best, the big man hadn't seemed to enjoy Mary's ministrations, and he'd hurt her. She knew he was the boss and that it was important to please him, so she was worried and scared.

'Everything all right, sir?' she hoped he would rot in hell sooner rather than later but in the meantime she needed him to be happy.

'Get dressed and go. You did well.'

*****

The week before Marion and Val were due to leave flew by, much to Val's consternation. She'd seen Gary every day and they'd had opportunities to be intimate, but had always been scuppered by some unexpected incident – from the sudden appearance of a snake, a bleeding mad dog and another freak storm. Val knew it was the guilt that made her feel that Ron was deliberately trying to stop her from sleeping with Gary, but nonetheless she couldn't shake off the feeling. It didn't help during her intimate moments with Gary, especially on the last occasion when a mirror had fallen off the wall and smashed into smithereens.

For his part, Gary became more and more frustrated. The harder Val was to attain the more he wanted her. The biggest loser in the scenario was Mary. Every time he came to her he was more cruel and violent and she came to fear the words *get ready, the boss wants to see you.* She had tried to tempt him with drinks, knowing it would be easier if she could drug him. He'd always declined and just wanted to use and abuse her body but never seemed to get any pleasure from it. Mary was baffled and frightened. When the housemaster had spoken to the boss he'd ended up with a nose spread all over his face and a black eye. If he could do that to him, what hope did she have? She didn't know how much more her mind or body could take but also knew there was no hope of escape, no hope of rescue, simply no hope.

*****

The day of departure had arrived and Val said goodbye to Marion who had opted to get a taxi to the airport. 'So you and your boyfriend can say goodbye in private.'

She'd come across as sincere and Val was grateful both for the fact that Marion was understanding and also that she would be able to spend a few hours with Gary before leaving the country.

The journey to the airport was subdued. Neither wanting to separate, but current circumstances not allowing otherwise. They'd talked about Val staying with Gary but he was transient, due to his work he told Val, so that wasn't a possibility. In addition, they didn't want to make any firm arrangements until they'd taken their relationship to the logical next step.

'It's been like we're jinxed for the past week,' Val was looking out of the window and the words had just slipped out.

'Shall we pull over here?' Gary was hopeful when she turned to look at him. They heard an almighty roar and instead of being frightened, they both laughed as he floored the accelerator and headed out of the bush back toward civilisation, as fast as the Land Rover would take them.

Their farewell at the airport was sad and emotional. After check-in they hugged and Val cried. Gary felt panic welling up inside at the thought of not seeing her again.

'I love you,' he said, 'and I want us to be together, whatever it takes.'

She was taken aback and caught up in the moment. 'I love you too, Gary. Please come to England.'

'I will my love, as soon as I can tie up a few loose ends here. We're meant to be together,' he knew it would be difficult and dangerous, but he was determined not to lose this woman.

They kissed for one final time, a bittersweet moment that was full of urgent desperation, rather than passion. The trickle of tears had turned into a torrent by this stage and Val wiped her face with the back of the sleeve on her safari jacket, laughing embarrassingly.

'Keep in touch,' he said as they broke apart and she couldn't bear it any more. Why hadn't she slept with him when she'd had the chance? Why hadn't she told him she loved him before? Why did she have to go?

Neither wanted to be the first to leave and Marion watched as the minutes ticked by. She didn't want them to miss the flight but neither did she want to be the one to break up the party. Their flight was called and Marion was relieved that the Tannoy announcement had done the job for her. This is going to be a fun trip she thought to herself. She wasn't looking forward to the sixteen-hour journey, but with Val being emotional about leaving her boyfriend whom Marion despised, it would seem even longer and less enjoyable.

They changed at Johannesburg and freshened up during the two-hour wait before boarding the next flight. They took off just before 9pm and Val had started to calm down by then. Emotionally drained, she slept for most of the second part of the journey and Marion was relieved that she didn't have to make small talk and be two-faced about how good a bloke Gary was. By the time they touched down just after 5am, they were exhausted, despite the fact that both had slept for a fair part of the journey. As far as Marion was concerned, she could have a full night's sleep on a plane and she'd still feel done in. There was something unnatural about flying but at least the time difference was only one hour so hopefully she'd feel better within a day or two.

The twins, Libby and Fiona were at the airport to meet them. Even though she was excited to see her mother after all this time and nervous about how she'd react to their news, Libby could tell that something wasn't quite right between the two women.

'They've fallen out.'

'Don't be ridiculous,' said Tony, and when Fiona raised her eyebrows, Libby elaborated.

'Look at their body language, it's almost as if they can't stand to be near each other. And they're not smiling or laughing and joking.'

'I can't see it either,' said Jim. 'They've been travelling for nearly 24 hours, they must be absolutely shattered. I don't think anyone would be full of the joys.'

'We'll see.' Fiona gave Libby a knowing look. The twins could pick-up on each other's emotions and of course their sister's, but couldn't see or sense the subtle nuances of body language between the two female friends.

Watching both her own mother and Tony's wheel their cases towards the meeting area, Libby started to get nervous. Her bravado about how her mother wouldn't mind that she'd married while she was in Zambia was starting to desert Libby. She was about to start chewing a nail when Tony took the hand and squeezed it. He can certainly pick up my body language, thought Libby as she imagined that her husband felt pretty much the same as she did.

Marion saw them first and waved furiously. Forgetting about Val, she weaved and dodged through the other passengers eager to get to her sons and keen to hear about the progression of Jim and Fiona's wedding plans.

'Come here!' she dropped her case to the floor and hugged each son in turn as if they were 5 years old again, also babbling about how good it was to be back and to see them all. Fiona's hug wasn't quite as enthusiastic and Val and Libby were holding each other for a long time before Marion was able to say hello to her, unknown to her, new daughter-in-law.

Tony and Libby had agreed to wait until the time was right before telling their mothers the news but that didn't go quite to plan. Val was emotional and blurted out that Marion had dreamt that the youngsters had married. An immediate silence followed as if a fairy had waved a magic wand and stopped time.

'Tony?' asked Marion and he looked at his wife. They'd both removed their wedding rings on arrival at the airport and Val watched as her daughter rubbed her wedding ring finger as she moved to Tony's side.

'Oh no...'

'It's good news, Mum, and we're going to have a proper blessing so you haven't missed anything really.'

'Haven't missed anything. Haven't missed...'

'Val, let's hear what they have to say,' Marion interrupted and put a restraining arm on Val's.

She shook Marion's arm off none too gently. 'Keep out of this you. This is between me and my daughter.'

They were all surprised at the venom in the words and the twins knew for sure that Libby had been right about the fall out.

'But Tony's my son,' Marion stated the obvious. 'This is my family's business too,' she turned to her son. 'Tony?'

Val couldn't believe this. She was missing the man she quite possibly wanted to spend the rest of her life with. She had hoped for a safe and loving homecoming from her children. Her son was away with his mates and her daughter had decided to marry while she was away helping orphans, and hadn't even thought to discuss it with her.

'I want to talk to you,' it was the tone of voice that Val had used when Libby had committed a serious childhood offence and she squealed as her mother put her hand around her wrist in a vice-like grip and attempted to drag her away. Tony was having none of it and he grabbed Libby's other arm. People stopped to watch as poor Libby was pulled in an emotional and literal tug of war.

'Let her go!' Fiona's command shocked them all and Libby reeled backwards at the suddenness of her release. Jim stopped her from toppling over and Tony was instantly at her side, holding her and trying to stop her shaking.

'Look, shall we go for a drink and talk about this like adults?'

'How can you expect me to treat you like adults when you've behaved like children?' said Val looking to Marion for support. Marion wasn't as angry as Val. Sure, she was upset that they hadn't told her the plans beforehand but she was pleased for them both and they were planning a blessing so it wasn't the end of the world. She would have a proper talk with Tony later but for now she did not want to fall out with her sons after just touching down on English soil.

'I think we should go for a coffee, Val. Let them explain things.'

'I might have known you wouldn't support me on this.' Val retrieved her bags and stomped off.

'Mum, please don't. Mum, Mum!' Libby went after her mother in tears but Val refused to have anything to do with her daughter. Tony put his hand around his wife's waist and she sobbed into his shoulder. He'd worried that this was how it would turn out but Libby hadn't listened. Saying *I told you so* would be absolutely pointless so he comforted her until the tears subsided.

'She'll come round and we'll all laugh at this in years to come.'

Libby rolled her eyes in *yeah right* fashion and they slowly made their way to the cars.

'Welcome to the family, Libby,' said Marion as she got into the car with Jim and Fiona. 'But don't think you've got away with this completely, either of you.' Were her last words before she closed the door.

Feeling like naughty children, Tony and Libby waited for Jim's car to pull away before they looked at each other and burst out laughing, more to release the tension than in hilarity.

Claire, Ron and Sandy had watched the shenanigans at the airport and then split up – Ron and Sandy going with Val and seeing that her own mother was more or less okay about the nuptials, Claire decided to follow Tony and Libby.

Recalling the look on her mother's face it wasn't long before Libby's laughter turned to tears. She wiped them away angrily, not completely understanding her mother's reaction.

'I remember telling her that when I met the man of my dreams, I only wanted a small do without any fuss. She said *whatever you want my darling, you shall have*, and now she's surprised and acting all hurt. I don't understand it.'

Tony wondered if his wife were thinking out loud or talking to him as she turned her head to look out of the window. They were moving slowly on the

M25 so the view was mainly of other cars and drivers as they crawled along.

'Dirty pig,' said Libby laughing as she pointed to a driver carrying out a major excavation with his index finger in a nostril.

Christ, her mood's all over the place thought Tony, he'd have to tread carefully.

'How old were you when you had that discussion with your mother?'

'It wasn't just once, Tony. We talked about it loads of times.'

'Well. Maybe she thought you weren't being serious. After all, don't all girls want to be treated like a princess on their special day?'

Apparently not if Libby's look was anything to go by. She harrumphed and turned to face him.

'Don't be so bloody patronising!' she scowled and Tony could see that she was winding up for a biggie. 'This is the 21st century and what women actually want is to be equal partners, not whisked off somewhere by a knight in shining armour. I thought you knew I was independent when...'

'Right, enough. Please, darling,' their exit was coming up. Tony checked the traffic, indicated and they both remained quiet until he'd pulled off the motorway and onto an A road. Libby was simmering quietly in the passenger seat, needing to take her guilt out on someone he assumed.

Giving her a chance to calm down he drove for a few minutes then noticed a sign for a truck stop and refreshments. He pulled in and parked.

'I'm sorry. It just upset me seeing her like that. I guess it was too much of a surprise and I should have said something before she came home,' she started crying again.

Another mood change but this time Tony was relieved his wife had decided not to take it out on him, so he let the earlier comments pass. He reached across but the hug was awkward with the gear stick and handbrake in the way. They decided to get out of the car and have a coffee and leg stretch while they thought about how they could make it up to Val.

The cafe owner turned to look at Tony as he mumbled, 'now's not a good time, Claire.' There was nobody with the customer and Tony didn't make eye contact with the man who turned back to his machine and carried on preparing their drinks. When Libby had finished the call to her brother to explain what had happened, the man served their coffees and tapped his nose and winked at Tony as he heard him say *Are you all right Libby?*

'What was that about?' she asked and her husband shrugged his shoulders seemingly none the wiser than she was.

*****

Val slammed the door behind her and gave the house the quick once over. There were basic provisions in the cupboard and the fridge and the house looked clean and tidy. Libby had done something right she thought as she dragged her bags upstairs. Thinking of what her daughter had done upset her and she cried while she closed the curtains and undressed. The tears eventually dried up and, both physically and emotionally drained Val got into her freshly made bed. She closed her eyes and tried to work out why Libby had thought she wouldn't be upset about the wedding. Even though she'd slept on the plane, the tiredness eventually took hold and Val drifted off. It was early evening by the time she awoke and Val had a long shower then looked at the bags on the floor. She emptied them and sorted her belongings into piles for washing, wanting to sanitise absolutely everything that she'd brought back from Africa. On autopilot she hooked up to the Internet and ordered some of her favourite foods from Tesco, then made herself a coffee. Her thoughts turned to Libby again and she recalled the conversations they'd had throughout the years about Libby's future wedding. Val always thought that when Libby met her Mr Right she would want a big wedding. She now realised that her daughter had been deadly serious when she'd said otherwise and she wondered why she hadn't thought so at the time; after all, they'd talked about weddings on more than one occasion. Maybe it was because she'd expected her father to give her away so Val always assumed they would both be there and she'd be able to talk her into having a big wedding. What if Libby was punishing her for what she'd done to her father? Or maybe punishing her because she'd gone away and decided to get on with her own life? Maybe that's why Carl had arranged to be away too, because he wanted to punish her as well? She should have taken her daughter's comments seriously and then it wouldn't have been such a shock. The doorbell stopped her negative stream of thoughts and Val dried her eyes as she went to collect her groceries.

'Surprise!'

Her hand rushed to her mouth when she saw her son on the doorstep. Looking tanned and relaxed he'd be a fine catch for any girl thought his mother as he picked her up and swung her around before returning her to the doorstep and giving her a big hug. Val started to feel better as Carl followed her into the house.

Ron was very concerned about his wife and knowing how vulnerable she was at that moment worried him. She would be more susceptible to the advances of Gary and Ron was only too glad that there were thousands of miles between them. He was proud that his son had cut short his holiday to offer Val some moral support and realised that as parents, they had done something right to produce two such great adults. Ron understood Val's upset at the wedding but also understood Libby's logic too. He wondered how Val would feel if she'd known he'd been there and was just glad that she would never find out.

*****

Two days later and Libby was frustrated and upset that her mother still refused to take her calls. They'd met with Marion who was staying at Jim's flat with Jim and Fiona. She'd told them that she was disappointed that they hadn't thought to invite their mothers to the wedding. She'd finished by saying that she would forgive them only if they arranged a suitable and fitting occasion for the blessing. When Libby had asked what might be fitting, Marion had said that being Val's only daughter, it would be appropriate to discuss it with her mother and that they could let Marion know when arrangements had been made. Both Tony and Libby left Jim's flat feeling as if they'd just had a dressing down from a very disappointed head teacher and that they should now go away and try harder. Despite the dressing down, Libby knew that she and Tony's mother would get along just fine and that the current situation was merely a hiccup. She was worried that the future would not be so rosy with her own mother.

After many more calls Libby knew the only way to get through to her mother was by giving her an ultimatum.

'Right, Carl, I've had enough. I'll hold on while you go and tell Mum that this is the last time I'm calling. I want to come and talk to her and if she says no, that's it.'

'Don't say that, Libby. You know you don't mean it.'

100

'But I do.'

Val was flicking a duster around and couldn't help but overhear her son's part of the conversation. She sensed the tension and urgency and knew that she'd need to speak to Libby soon or risk losing her for good.

'Tell her to come round tonight. You and Tony can go for a pint while we talk.'

Carl conveyed the message to his sister and she breathed a sigh of relief, knowing that her mother would eventually forgive her if she played her cards right.

Chapter 9

Gary missed Val more than he'd expected. It made him feel weak and vulnerable and this annoyed him. Like a wasp with a headache, Gary's bad mood had ramifications for all those he came into contact with. Mary was used and abused and his staff avoided him as much as they could, too frightened to go to him with problems or questions. All Gary wanted was to see Val as soon as possible, to explore her body at long last, to laugh and joke with her, touch her, smell her...

He knew that going back to England was a risky business, even though nobody would recognise him for the man he used to be, but Gary didn't want to take too many risks. Some of his old contacts in Western Europe had been after exotic young girls for quite a while and he knew he could make a fortune from them. If his plan came to fruition, he could also arrange to pick up some more girls on the way. He started to make the arrangements and his staff noticed a marked change in their boss. From moody to determined they knew that nothing would get in the way of his plans when he wanted to bring an idea to fruition.

*****

Tony had elected to drop Libby off and visit his brother. They didn't see so much of each other these days. Fiona was going out with her mates and their mother had gone to Yorkshire for a few days to meet up with some old school friends that she'd reconnected with through Facebook, so it seemed like an ideal opportunity for a catch-up. He'd said hi to Carl and politely refused his invitation to the pub. He helped Libby inside with the massive bouquet she'd bought for her mother. The welcome was lukewarm to say the least but Tony had apologised for their actions and said he hoped she would eventually forgive them so that they could move forward as a family. Feeling like Ban Ki-moon must have before attempting to broker a deal between two opposing sides, Tony decided to leave them to it now the scene was set. Carl followed Tony and gave him a man hug before thanking him for grovelling to his mother.

'I know the wedding was Libby's idea and you just went along with it, mate, so you shouldn't have had to do that,' they were at the front door and Tony was more than ready to leave.

'Small price to pay if it helps to smooth the way.'

Carl nodded and the men shook hands. Tony got into his car and made his way to his brother's, feeling a little cowardly for leaving his wife to face the music alone, but also glad to be out of the firing line.

Enjoying the football and their catch up the twins stopped what they were doing at the same time and a knowing look passed between them.

'You could have waited until half-time,' said Jim as both men looked upwards.

Claire wondered why they always looked skyward, no matter where she was. She was actually looking out of the window and had tried to be patient but it wasn't really in her nature, so she'd let them know she was paying a visit.

'Glad to see that Mum didn't take it too badly.'

They made polite conversation for a few minutes before Claire sensed that they were waiting for her real reason for visiting.

'It's not particularly good news but I need your help.'

'Go on,' they were both intrigued and had temporarily forgotten about the match.

'Remember the guy who kidnapped Mel?'

'Of course,' said Tony. 'I remember the poor woman he murdered as well. I know it's frustrating for Dad and Mel that he hasn't been found yet. They're getting on with their lives but there's always that niggling doubt that he may turn up and...'

'He has,' interrupted Claire. 'But he's thousands of miles away just now but we don't know how long for.'

'What do you mean "we"?'

'Never mind that,' said Jim. 'Where is he and what do you expect him to do?'

His question was met with silence, but the twins could sense Claire's presence and knew she hadn't left. Now that the time had come for her to tell her brothers that the man who had kidnapped their half-sister, was likely to be shagging Tony's mother-in-law in the near future, Claire was delaying the bad news.

'Claire, what else is there?'

She knew they would be shocked and hoped they could help.

'Big Ed has changed his name to Gary Jamieson and he turned up in Zambia...'

The twins didn't like the sound of this.

'...at the orphanage where Mum and Val worked. He has a building business in the area but is up to his old tricks as well.'

'What do you mean, Claire? Does he know Mum and Val? Is he still grooming young girls?'

'All of the above,' she paused. 'There's no easy way to say this but him and Val are, well you know.'

'Oh my God,' said Tony. 'How am going to tell Libby. We have to call the police, Interpol or something. Can you track him Claire? Do you know where he is? We could get him arrested and extradited. Do they have an extradition treaty...'

'Whoa, hang on a minute,' she hadn't meant to be so loud and the curtains shook and the door slammed shut, shocking the twins.

'Jesus, was that you, Claire?'

They calmed down when they heard her giggles. 'Wow, I didn't know I could do that. I'm almost as impressed are you are.'

Knowing their sister as they did, they listened patiently as other doors around the flat closed, the blind banged against the window in the kitchen and open windows blew shut. She was obviously trying out her newfound tricks and eventually she returned to the conversation.

'Sorry about that. A bit frivolous I know but I just couldn't help myself. Have you had time for the news to sink in now?'

Seeing them both nod, she carried on. 'Gary, Big Ed, whatever you want to call the man, has had cosmetic surgery so his face isn't recognisable. He is very dangerous. I can tell you that it's not always possible for us... me I mean, to keep track of him.'

'Why's that?'

Claire hadn't been told not to tell them about the evil spirits and, in fact, wanted them to be aware so that if the time came, they wouldn't take any unnecessary risks.

'He's being accompanied by some very unsavoury characters, not of your world. You know that I can now do a few tricks. Well, his soul mates are evil and are also able to perform certain tricks which makes keeping a track on him a risky business.'

'So you're telling us that there's a chance that this guy and Libby's Mum might already be sleeping together and he might be grooming young girls, and there's nothing we can do about it?'

'Not exactly,' said Claire. 'Firstly, I don't think they have slept together yet which is good news. I probably shouldn't be telling you this but Val wasn't quite ready to start the physical side of their relationship. Secondly, girls have gone missing from the orphanage but no boys. We're going to try and find out more information and keep you informed.'

'So what do you want us to do?' asked Tony.

'He's really keen on Val. We think he might try to visit her. You need to keep her away from him if he does. See, it's not much to ask is it?'

'And what am I supposed to tell Libby?'

'Easy. Now she's a believer you can tell her the truth. The more people looking out for Val, the better. Oh, and the good news is that Mum met him and took an instant dislike to him. She's quite perceptive, our mother.'

The twins were relieved that their mother hadn't been taken in by the evil charmer.

'But what about telling the police?'

'You can do that if you can think of a plausible reason for how you've got hold of this information.'

Fair point thought both men. Neither of them could come up with a good reason to explain how they'd found out about this man and even if they told the police about the girls going missing, they were sure that they'd be told it was a national and not an international crime.

'Best not to mention any of this to Mum and Dad either,' Claire moved an ornament to regain their attention.

'For Christ sake, stop that! You're freaking us out,' said Jim and Claire giggled for a few seconds before turning serious.

'I don't want to worry the rest of the family unnecessarily. If he arrives in this country that might change, but you can tell Fiona,' Claire had anticipated Jim's next question. 'Libby may need her help and support.'

The twins were mulling over the information passed to them by Claire as she said a quick goodbye and disappeared.

'It sounds to me like there's a battle between good and evil going on in her world,' said Jim. 'So she can't be in heaven yet, can she?'

His brother was thinking exactly the same thing and none of it yet made any sense to either of them.

*****

Marion was on the train to London on her way back from Yorkshire. She'd contacted *People Against Poverty* during a quiet moment at the hotel and had initially spoken to Gail. Gail had carried out the volunteer training for Marion and Val and both women were now friends with the easy-going trainer. Marion hadn't meant to share her worries with Gail but once she'd started telling her concerns about Daniel, all the other stuff had come out and by the end of the call, she'd felt relieved that she'd been able to share her problems and that Gail hadn't thought she was making something out nothing. Marion knew deep down to trust her own instincts but Val's reaction had made her doubt herself. Gail had obviously trusted her judgement as Marion had just hung up on a call asking that she and Val visit the charity HQ the following day at 10 am. They must be very concerned she thought, to respond to her call at 7pm and convene a meeting for the next morning. She wasn't looking forward to calling Val to tell her about the meeting, but they had to try and sort something out soon thought Marion, if they were going to work on the orphanage project together in Romania.

*****

Carl had made them tea before retreating to the pub and Val had thanked Libby for the flowers. The two women now sat opposite each other, Val on the green leather settee, and Libby on one of the matching armchairs. She took a deep breath.

'I don't know how many more times to say I'm sorry. I didn't expect you to be so upset especially when you knew I didn't want a big wedding.'

They'd been around this buoy already but Libby felt the need to repeat herself.

'You are my only daughter, Libby. I wanted to show you off to all our family and friends at your wedding, so that everyone knows how proud I am and how much you mean to me,' she wiped away the tears with the back of her hand. 'And now I'll never have that chance.'

'Oh, Mum.' Libby put down her mug and moved to her mother and hugged her.

'But why didn't you tell me this when we talked about weddings?'

'Because I didn't want to say I thought I could talk you round. As you didn't have a serious boyfriend at the time I...' They were quiet for a moment while Val gathered her thoughts.

'I expected you to meet someone and come home one day and say it was serious. Then get carried away with me about planning your wedding and then you'd change your mind and say you wanted a big do, a dress with a long train, reception, the works. Your father and I have been putting a bit away for years for yours and Carl's wedding you know.'

Libby wasn't aware of their wedding funds and up until a few minutes before hadn't realised that she could actually feel guiltier than she already did.

'I'm so sorry, Mum,' now they were both crying and hugging. 'It would have been hard without Dad there to give me away too. Please say you'll forgive me?' This wasn't the time to tell her mother about the message from her father, perhaps there would never be a right time.

Val wiped a tear from her daughter's face and pulled her to her. She stroked her hair and Libby enjoyed the closeness to her mother, which she hadn't had for ages.

'I do feel hurt, Libby, but I'll get over it. Especially if you and Tony do decide to have a proper blessing and invite lots of friends and family, have a reception, a beautiful dress, maybe a piper and some beautiful photographs...'

Libby laughed. How could she deny her mother this after seeing how upset she'd been?

Now that the bridge between mother and daughter had been fixed, Val was keen to tell Libby about some of her experiences in Zambia. Libby already knew a little of the country from the tales her mother had told her the first time she'd gone away with Marion. Val gradually added Gary into the anecdotes and Libby noticed her mother's eyes sparkle when she talked about this new mystery man.

'Ooh, he sounds interesting. Is he good to you?'

'Very.'

'And is he good looking.'

Val laughed, embarrassed. 'Very,' she turned serious. 'Do you think it's too soon, Libby? It's platonic up to now but that may very well change.'

Libby wasn't used to seeing her mother blush and tried not to show that she'd noticed. 'Mum, Dad's been gone for just over two years now. You loved each other but I'm sure he'll understand.'

'You mean he would have understood?'

'Yes, that's exactly what I meant. You have to be sure that it's what you want though, Mum. I don't want you to be hurt by this man.'

'If you knew him you'd know he'd never hurt me, Libby. I really miss him and can't wait to see him again.'

'When's that likely to happen?'

Val explained that Gary had been in touch and was hoping to do some business in Europe. He was trying to arrange his dates so that it coincided with her break, halfway through her next tour in Romania, or at the end of that tour. The phone went and Libby listened to her mother's discussion. She got the impression that it was Marion but still didn't know her mother's reason for their falling out.

'What's happened between you two?' Libby asked as soon as her mother had rung off and Val explained that Marion was jealous of her new relationship with the charming and good-looking Gary.

'Ooh. I never knew Tony's Mum was like that.'

Val explained that she had doubts about whether they could work together in Romania and told Libby about the meeting at the charity HQ the following morning.

'I really want to do this job in Romania but they've said they want us as a package. So I'm going to be grown-up and try and put what happened in Zambia behind us. I don't want Marion to know when and I where I'm meeting Gary though, that part of my life is none of her business.'

Libby thought it was sad that there was a tear in the friendship and hoped that it could be mended. It was a shame as they had been inseparable before their latest tour to Zambia and that closeness had meant that Carl and Libby worried about their mother a lot less than they used to. She wondered if she were being selfish in hoping that her mother and mother-in-law would regain that close friendship again in the not too distant future.

Tony came to pick Libby up a little later and she wondered why he hadn't seemed really pleased that her relationship with her mother was almost back to normal.

'Are you okay? You seem preoccupied.'

'Can we wait until we're home and then we'll talk?'

He hadn't said that everything was fine and Libby didn't have a good feeling about what was to come later.

'There's no easy way to tell you this, sweetheart,' he pushed her gently into the lounge and she sat down.

Libby knew that nobody had died, but Tony looked so solemn and worried, she was scared.

'Whatever it is. Just tell me!'

'Your mother's seeing someone new, and that man...'

'Oh, I see. You've been talking to your mother and she's told you her version of events. My mother said your mother's jealous of her new bloke and that's why they've fallen out. Apparently he's really good looking and charming and is kind and thoughtful as well and...' her words trailed off and she stopped when she saw the look on her husband's face. 'What?'

'Do you want a drink?'

'I just want to know what's going on here?'

'Libby. The man your mother is falling for is the one who kidnapped my step sister.'

'WHAT!' this time it was a scream. 'Don't be ridiculous, his picture was all over the papers, she's been in Zambia, not on another planet. Has your mother told you that?'

'I don't know why you keep talking about my mother, this is nothing to do with her...'

'But I thought she told you, nobody else knows about my mother seeing this man called Gary.'

'He's changed his name to Gary Jamieson, Libby. He used to be known as *Big Ed* and has had cosmetic surgery to change his appearance. He's a murderer and grooms young girls to have sex with older men. He's evil, Libby and we have to protect your mother.'

'Oh my God,' she put her hand over her mouth finding it difficult to take in the information. A few seconds later she realised something didn't quite ring true. 'Hang on a minute. How do you know all this? Who told you if it wasn't your mother?'

Libby saw the look on her husband's face and realised what must have happened. 'So she came to talk to you when you were with Jim?'

'Yup.'

Before she'd received a message from the Medium Michael Gray, Libby didn't believe that their dead sister was really communicating with them. She thought it was their way of handling the grief. Now she was in no doubt that the departed could contact some of those on the living plain, but still found Tony's revelation a bit of a stretch.

'So let me get this right. Your sister has been to Zambia watching your mother, sorry, her mother as well, and my mother. And, even though that guy has apparently had cosmetic surgery, she recognised him as the man who kidnapped your stepsister and murdered another woman. Is that about right?'

'Hmm, hm.'

'So, sorry to state the obvious, but how did she recognise him?'

Tony could see her point and wished they'd asked Claire more questions.

A gust of wind blew the curtains and they billowed as if someone big was standing behind them trying to hide.

'Tell her that the woman he murdered was with us,' shouted Claire.

'What the hell?' screamed Libby.

'Will you stop doing that,' shouted Tony.

'Tony, it's freaking me out, what's happening?' she was visibly shaking and all colour had drained from her face. It was only Claire and Tony didn't understand why his wife was so frightened until he tried to put himself in her shoes. Yup, he'd be crapping it too. He took her in his arms and held her until she'd calmed down.

'It's all right, sweetheart. Nobody's going to hurt you. Umm, Claire's discovered that she can do new things and she forgets that it frightens some of us.'

'Claire, stop it now and calm down.'

It wasn't a request and Claire momentarily forgot that she had the upper hand and automatically did what one of her big brothers told her to.

'Right. If you frighten Libby again, you're banned from visiting when Libby's about and if you do, I will ignore you, no matter how difficult that may be.'

He's talking to the ceiling again thought Claire who was hovering by the television.

'Okay, sorry.'

'She said sorry.'

'This is effing weird,' said Libby shaking her head.

'Tell Libby that her father and Sandy, the woman Big Ed murdered, were watching her mother and Sandy twigged that it was Big Ed who was with her.'

The message passed, Libby accepted the information. 'And is err, Sandy 100 per cent sure?' Now she was talking to the ceiling.

'Absolutely no doubt about it,' Claire replied. 'Our, umm, bosses double-checked and confirmed it.'

Claire sensed another presence and looked around. She was relieved to see it was Raphael and he was beckoning her with his finger.

'I can't talk anymore I've got to go. I'll be in touch.'

Tony knew that she was gone as soon as she'd passed her final message and he took his wife's hand and they walked to the kitchen. He got two glasses out of the cupboard and went to pour brandy into both.

'I may have had a shock but there's no way I'm drinking that stuff. It's horrible.'

He breathed a sigh of relief. She was going to be okay. Mixing her usual poison of vodka and tonic they returned to the lounge to discuss what had happened, and what to do to protect her mother from the clutches of Gary Jamieson.

Chapter 10

They were coming in from different directions so Val and Marion had arranged to meet at 9am at a coffee shop in Victoria station, and walk the ten minutes or so to the charity HQ together. Marion had just finished her coffee and stood up as Val arrived. They hugged and although it was a little awkward, both women realised they'd missed each other's friendship and company.

'I'm sorry,' said Marion.

'Me too.'

They hugged again and this time it felt like the most natural thing in the world.

'Have you spoken to Libby?'

'Yes and they're going to do the blessing but it's going to be like a big wedding. They'll make sure that it's when we're not away and she said she'd love my opinion on the arrangements.'

Marion smiled and acted surprised at the news, even though Tony had phoned her and told her about Libby and Val's reconciliation.

They linked arms to cross the road, both comfortable again in each other's company. Val decided that this was the way ahead and that they could get along just fine if she didn't bring Gary into the equation. As long as Marion didn't put him down, she would accept this. Gail met them at reception.

'Hiya. Great to see you both. Wow, how much weight have you lost?' She looked at them both with a beaming smile and Marion felt a huge surge of warmth for this woman. They kissed and hugged then headed for the lift. Gail turned serious.

'Mr Donaldson is away on business. Funnily enough he's in Eastern Europe overseeing the preparations for a number of new projects, including your next one.'

'Who are we seeing?' asked Val.

'Sylvia, Mr Donaldson's deputy and she's asked me to sit in too.'

'Sorry if you had plans for today,' said Marion. 'But I thought...' Val gave her a look. 'We mulled it over and thought it was important.'

'No worries. I don't have a life.' They laughed with relief when they realised that Gail was joking.

The introductions over and coffee served – instant because Sylvia didn't call her Secretary in at weekends – Sylvia asked for an overview of their tour. She noticed how the women finished each other's sentences like an old married couple. They had done well and worked well together. However, Gail had told her about the disagreement and the presumed death of the girls and it was this that Sylvia wanted to discuss.

'So you were informed that a rogue lion had taken the three girls?' both women nodded.

'When Mary disappeared,' said Marion. 'I saw a white vehicle pass me as I was collecting water. It could only have been to the orphanage but when I spoke to Daniel about it he denied it and acted as if he were up to something. I couldn't put my finger on what exactly but I don't believe a lion took those girls, I think there's something sinister going on there.'

Sylvia noticed the subtle changes in Val's demeanour and her slight movement away from Marion. She had information she couldn't share with the women and would have to play this very carefully.

'But a lion was killed and caught and nobody else has gone missing since?'

'Exactly,' said Val sitting up and bursting with enthusiasm. 'You may have heard of the help the orphanage has received from Gary Jamieson? Well, he arranged a hunting party and brought back the lion and also erected a fence to help protect the children.'

'Admirable.' said Sylvia and Marion saw the quick look that passed between Gail and Sylvia and wondered what they were hiding.

'Gary's employed locally, Val. Do you know him well?'

Val blushed at the question. 'We're getting to know each other, and hoping to meet up on my first break from Romania. Why do you ask?'

'Because if there's something illegal going on, we must ensure that there are no negative implications for People Against Poverty,' she leaned forward. 'Are you sure you can trust this man?'

'Look, Sylvia. For the record Marion and I disagree on this but we can still work together without this coming between us.' Sylvia looked at Marion who nodded.

'Gary is a kind, thoughtful man who only wants to protect people and give something back to society. I'm all for an investigation and agree with Marion that Daniel's not the right person to have at the orphanage. He's egotistical, selfish and unhelpful. He doesn't have the interests of the children at heart and if anything illegal is happening, it's down to him and Gary doesn't know anything about it.'

She's got it bad thought Sylvia. 'Well thanks, ladies. I'll speak to the Director on his return next week and we'll decide on the way ahead. Now, do you have any questions or concerns about Romania?'

They had a discussion about the next project and the meeting ended. Gail started to escort them to the lift and Val excused herself to use the ladies.

'What's going on?' asked Marion when Val was out of earshot.

'I don't know what you mean?'

'I'm not stupid, Gail,' Marion whispered urgently. I know something's going on that you haven't told us about, and if you don't tell me I'm going to call the Director.

'I'm not exactly sure myself. Call me later and I'll tell you what I can.'

They heard the climp clomp of Val's heels and the conversation moved onto the weather and shopping while Gail booked the visitors out of the building.

Sylvia looked out of the window at the people down below, going about their business like little ants, but not in as much of a hurry as the weekday crowds. She turned when she heard Gail enter her office.

'Well?'

'Marion knows something's up and she's going to call me later. Why didn't you tell them?'

'The police called while you were meeting them. I've got to call them back but the gist of the conversation was that Gary Jamieson isn't who he seems. They're working with Interpol to investigate international sex slavery involving children,' she pulled her fingers down her cheeks and shook her head. 'They think he's involved and so is the local police chief.'

'You're kidding!'

'I wish I was. And it doesn't take a genius to work out that it wasn't a lion that took those girls from one of our orphanages.'

'Shit.'

'I couldn't have put it better myself.'

'But why didn't you tell them?'

'Because Gary Jamieson and our very own Daniel Mulenga have disappeared and the police may want to use Val to find Gary. As we speak they're trying to obtain a warrant to track all her communications...'

'But...'

'But nothing, Gail. I've been told not to stop their deployment to Romania because the police can still track emails, calls and such and there's no way these guys would just fly out of the country. It's a complicated situation and bad enough that vulnerable children have disappeared while under the care of our charity. Damage limitation is that we cooperate with the authorities as much as we can.'

Sylvia looked to Gail as if she had aged considerably while they were speaking. 'Marion's not stupid and has threatened to speak to the Director. What do I tell her?'

It was obvious to both women that Marion and Val disagreed on all matters to do with Gary Jamieson.

'I know Marion, she's like a terrier and won't let this go. She could cause more harm than good if she keeps digging. I'll speak to the Director and he can speak to the police or make the decision. I don't get paid enough to have that responsibility.'

Gail could see how Sylvia had reached the position she was in, at such a young age.

'I'll let you know as soon as I've talked to him. In the meantime, try not to worry too much.'

Easier said than done thought Gail deciding to delay the shopping that she'd planned earlier. This was too big for even retail therapy to conquer.

He wasn't quite ready for the journey but had had to advance his plans. Daniel had visited his digs without invitation early that morning – a big no no as far as Gary was concerned until he'd heard the reason. He'd taken out his frustration on Daniel who was now sporting a black eye and a few bruised ribs. Daniel had told him that two white men in suits had escorted the Chief of Police into a big black car with tinted windows. Daniel had rushed home when he'd heard the news and told his wife to pack. He'd booked a flight out of the country for her and the children. He didn't tell Gary that she'd initially refused to go and he'd had to explain that he might end up in prison. That and the fact that she loved her rich lifestyle had convinced her and as far as he now knew, his family were safely on their way to Europe. Gary had been finalising plans all day and would have to stop later on, on the road to make sure that everything was in order with the ship and that he could swap the bus for more fresh young girls before they arrived at the port. They would travel overland to Angola and pick up the freighter in Luanda. The human cargo could be easily hidden amongst the scrap metal ship and the captain was well respected. This made travelling in the Atlantic round Equatorial Guinea, Nigeria, Senegal and many other dodgy countries less dangerous than he'd initially anticipated. Gary wasn't bothered about pirates. Along with the ship's captain, he'd hired the biggest bunch of mean mercenary bastards going and if local pirates wanted a go at them, good luck to them. They'd stop off in one or two places to stock up on provisions and if the opportunity arose to buy more girls, he'd be a fool not to take it. They'd eventually dock in Algiers and hopefully, when his business was finished, Val would be just about halfway through her Romanian tour and he'd be able to convince her to meet him somewhere other than England. He'd have plenty of time to think of a reason for being elsewhere on business.

He felt like shit and didn't want any of his staff to be aware of a potential illness. As far as Gary was concerned, if he couldn't control his own body there was no way he could be in control of others. He fought whatever it was that was attacking his system but the effort left him tired and drained and the responsibility of every decision made weighed on him like a pneumatic drill, forcing him further and further into the ground. By 11 o'clock that night they were all ready to leave and Gary's Land Rover was parked in front of the bus waiting for his human cargo to be loaded. He'd told Daniel to drive the Rover, hoping to catch up on some sleep and recharge his batteries during the journey, which would take at least 38 hours. He watched as the girls and their armed guards filed slowly onto the bus, and was surprised to see the smile on the face of young Mary when she noticed him in the passenger seat of his vehicle.

Mary saw her tormentor wipe the sweat from his brow with an old handkerchief. She hoped that this was the first sign that the disease was starting to take hold of him. Still not understanding why she was still alive and for the most part, unaffected by the dreadful virus that she was convinced she had, she assumed that it had something to do with her late father and the rest of her family and that at long last, karma was kicking-in. She'd locked eyes with the evil one and hoped that he hadn't seen into her soul because he would have known for sure that his days were numbered.

A push from one of the heavy guards brought Mary back to the present and she looked at the vehicle in front of her. Mostly green with black around the wheels and bumpers, the single decker bus had a single luggage rack on the roof. Mary noticed a man with a gun looking around from the top of the bus before she climbed the three wobbly steps to go inside. Even by her limited experience of modes of transport, her instinct told her that this vehicle was well passed its prime and she hoped that their journey would be a short one. She walked along the length of the bus. The seats were green and felt hard when she sat down. The material wasn't leather but Mary stuck to it within seconds of sitting. They weren't cushioned and there were no arm rests so they were all in for an uncomfortable ride. The guards and driver left the bus and went to talk to the men in the Land Rover. While the girls waited for their return they had a good look around. There were luggage racks above them and at least they could store their meagre belongings up there out of the way. Mary took some of her clothing out of her small bag, folded the items and sat on them to make the seat slightly more comfortable. The others soon followed suit. Mary noticed that the long back seat appeared to have been customised into a sleeping area and she looked at Tamara to see if she had noticed. Her friend's face showed that she was thinking the same thing.

'I hope we don't have to perform in front of each other,' Mary shrugged her shoulders. She shared the same hope. The indignities they suffered were bad enough in private, but if they had to commit the disgusting acts in front of all their friends, it would be horrendous. It was all right for her because she was the boss's favourite; in fact she was the only one he used. She was out of bounds to all the others and she knew they were all frightened of him and wouldn't risk his wrath.

The girls settled as the guards and driver returned to the bus. The Land Rover pulled off ahead of them and they followed. Within 30 minutes of the journey starting the Land Rover could only just be seen by the driver and girls at the front of the bus. One of the guards put his weapon on his seat and stretched. He got up and grabbed the girl nearest to him. She squealed as he dragged her to the back of the bus. She started shouting and sobbing as he ripped off her clothes none to gently.

Not knowing what possessed her Mary got up from her seat and called for the other girls to follow her. They weren't keen on this idea until she explained that they were at the whim of the guards and if they didn't do something straight away, any one of them could be next in line. Reluctantly the girls followed her one by one. Mary was shaking but determined.

'Leave her alone!'

Amazed. The guard lifted himself off the girl and pulled up his jeans. The other guard was making his way from the front to the back of the bus.

'Who the hell do you think you are?' he zipped up his jeans, threw back his hand and gave Mary a slap, which knocked her backwards. He moved toward her to hit her again. The others cowered and Mary was terrified but wasn't going to give in.

'If the boss asks me how I got that mark I'm going to tell him.'

The guard stopped in his tracks.

'I'm sure we'll be worth less money if we're damaged.'

The first guard stepped over Mary carefully and grabbed hold of the other one, whispering urgently into his ear.

So I'm right thought Mary. They aren't allowed to touch us. She knew she wasn't completely out of danger yet though.

'I won't say anything if you leave us alone.'

Mary received such a look from the partly clothed guard that she knew she'd made an enemy and would have to be very careful around him. The other man gave her a curious look, which she couldn't place and there seemed to be a twinkle in his eyes. He merely nodded his head and shoved his colleague back towards his seat. The girl in the back seat quickly dressed and on the way back to her seat put her arms around Mary and hugged her until Mary thought she'd be squeezed to death. The girls in the seats in front and behind her smiled and mouthed their thanks and Tamara kissed her on the cheek. She had gained their respect and although she was by no means the oldest or most experienced, had assumed the unwanted role of the leader of their group.

Daniel had started chatting as soon as they'd got into the Land Rover and Gary told him to *shut the fuck up* if he didn't want another black eye and a broken nose to go with it this time. Gary closed his eyes and the next time he opened them the sun was high in the sky and the animals and insects were well awake and making enough noise to wake the dead. He looked at his watch, 9 o'clock. He'd slept for 10 hours straight and still felt like absolute shit.

'Stop at the next village so we can have a break and some food.'

Daniel nodded. 'You all right boss?'

He looked like death to Daniel but there was no way that he'd tell him that. Gary could usually handle any situation but Daniel wondered if having to practically do a midnight flit had stressed him out.

'Fine. When we get to the village buy food and drink to eat there and some to take with us so we can stop where we want next time. When you negotiate, give them a good price on the understanding that they haven't seen us if anyone asks about us.'

'Yes, boss.' He should already be aware that people will give information to the highest bidder thought Daniel, but there was no way that he was going to tell him that. He wasn't sure he would on a good day, but in his current mood, no chance.

They arrived and Daniel asked to see the Village Elder. Negotiations commenced and the Village Elder could see that Gary had company that were invisible to others. He didn't like the man so kept his distance when Gary offered to shake his hand.

'He's superstitious of strangers,' Daniel quickly explained, not wanting the boss to go off on one.

Negotiations completed and the Village Elder had given his word that he would not tell any strangers about their visit. Some of the village women hurried around with bowls of food and water, which were wolfed down by both the children and adults. The guards kept a close watch on the girls to ensure that they didn't speak to the women, even accompanying them while they relieved themselves in the basic facilities. The villagers weren't stupid and knew that the young girls weren't with the men by choice. The Elder had told his senior wife that the women were not to ask questions and she had passed the word. There would be plenty of time for discussion after the strangers left.

Refreshed with full bellies and some dried food they left the village less than an hour after their arrival. Having consulted the map Gary reckoned their journey would take at least another 30 hours and that they'd overestimated how fast the bus could go. He put Daniel on the bus for the next leg of the journey and ordered the non-shifty looking guard to drive the Land Rover. He didn't like the look of the other one and told Daniel to keep an eye on him and to make sure he didn't touch the goods.

They stopped a few more times on the way, all too exhausted to marvel at the wonderful scenery en route. Even the girls who didn't know what their future held just wanted the journey to be over. The road on approach to the Angolan border was not a road at all, but a single lane sand track. Gary marvelled at the sturdy Bedford bus. The vehicle had tackled anything thrown at it and in a weird way he was often proud to be British, and wasn't surprised at the parts of the world his country had occupied in the past. The craftsmanship of the old bus was brilliant and he wasn't surprised when she took the sand track in her stride. They passed their papers to the border officials who were interested in the cargo until they found the sizeable bribe and no further questions were asked. He was glad that nobody in this part of the world seemed bothered about doing their job properly – his life would have been extremely difficult if they were.

After what seemed an age they arrived at the port in Luanda. Gary took in the scene around him - cranes as far as the eye could see lifting the containers off the freighters and onto land and vice versa. Who knew what was hidden in those containers and where they were headed. For the size of the port Gary imagined it was a twenty-four hour operation and he was correct. The ship's captain had explained that there were no overnight storage facilities but that his shipping company had some rooms in an old large disused Portakabin, and that the girls could be kept there safely from their arrival until their departure later on the same day. Gary had toyed with the idea of using the passenger terminal in Luanda and obtaining false identification documents for the girls. After weighing up the pros and cons he knew this idea was fraught with potential problems and that the best plan was the one he'd decided on. Luckily, one of his contacts in Europe had put him onto the ship's captain who was well connected locally. He quickly scanned the ships that were docked. Most of them were too big for what he'd expected but there were three that could be the one they were booked onto. Instead of guessing, Gary sent the guards to find the old captain and his scrap metal freighter. He also sent Daniel to find the man who was taking the bus. He'd negotiated 5 young girls in exchange for the bus and was amazed at how cheap life was. In the end he accepted 4, one had mysteriously disappeared and Gary didn't want to delay his journey or draw any further attention to himself while he waited for another to be procured. He concluded this part of his business in a rush, keen to get on the ship and summon Mary, to prove he wasn't losing his masculinity.

Chapter 11

Every time Marion tried to call Gail over the next five days she got her answering service. She was so annoyed but wasn't seeing Val until the following week when they were doing two days of familiarisation training before departing for Romania just three days later. Mulling over her time between jobs she thought that the twins were unusually quiet, but Fiona and Libby had been very interested in their Zambia tour and had asked loads of questions. They'd pumped her for information about that man but Marion hadn't wanted to worry Libby so had kept it as light as she could, and had tried her best to keep her opinions to herself. She knew that the girls knew she didn't like Gary, but guessed that Val had talked to Libby about him and her mother's side of the story would have been completely different from her own. She was running out of time and patience and contemplating whether to call the Director, as she was finishing her grocery shopping and packing the car. Her mobile rang and the display showed that it was Gail.

'Can we meet?' was Gail's hasty greeting and they arranged to meet at the charity headquarters the following day. 'Don't tell Val,' Gail added unnecessarily.

Marion had felt guilty for withholding information from the charity and wanted to be the first to speak. As soon as she sat down in the room with Sylvia and Gail and the secretary had served filtered coffee and green tea, she off loaded.

'I should have told you before but I found some bank statements in the office drawer,' she sucked in a breath. 'Gary had deposited two large sums into a UK bank account in Daniel's name.'

'Why didn't you tell us this before?'

'Sylvia, Val doesn't know about this. We had a major fallout over Gary and can get along just fine as long as neither of us talks about him. If I had told you that at our meeting, Val would have gone berserk and accused me of God only knows what.'

'Okay, we'll pass that information on to the police, they're already involved.'

Marion raised her eyebrows and Sylvia explained.

Although she had suspected that the men were involved in the abduction of the girls, to be told that Interpol were on their case and that they would be tracking Val's emails and listening to her phone calls was quite a revelation.

'Oh shit,' was Marion's uncharacteristic response.

'Shit indeed,' said Sylvia. 'The police have said not to change our plans for you ladies as that might alert Gary Jamieson, or whatever his real name is. Will you be able to carry on as if you don't know any of this, and keep it from Val for the time being?'

Marion thought for a moment. She had been spot on about both men and her and Val had already agreed not to talk about Gary.

'Whatever's happened between us Val is still my best friend... she's going to be devastated. Could you keep this from your best friend?'

'Marion,' Sylvia leaned forward. 'If you tell Val and she doesn't believe you, there's a chance she'll contact him and that could blow the whole police operation.'

'The police believe he's going to bring the girls to Europe and hope to catch him there,' said Gail. 'If he finds out, those girls may not be rescued and who knows what the rest of their lives will be like?'

It was a no brainer then. She had to think of the greater good of the girls who'd been kidnapped.

'Okay, I won't tell her. But this may well be the kiss of death for our friendship.'

Sylvia got up to signify that the meeting was over. They would usually have concluded with a formal handshake but this time the women hugged and Sylvia told Marion how grateful she was for her cooperation. She would see them both the following week and have a quick chat, ostensibly about the investigation of Daniel Mulenga and if there was any progress on that front. They said their goodbyes and Marion left, feeling as if she had the weight of the world on her shoulders.

Marion did a bit of shopping in London and tried to lift her mood before arriving back at the flat in time for dinner. She was surprised to see that both twins were there along with Libby and Fiona. Although Claire had told them not to tell their mother, the twins had decided to go against her wishes believing it would be in Val's best interest.

'Okay, what's going on?'

They all look so flaming serious thought Marion. After the day she'd had she could do without more devastating news. She mentally composed herself and thought of her daughter. To lose a child was the worst possible thing in life and went against the normal laws of nature. Marion had endured and was still enduring that agony so anything else life threw at her might be awful, but a doddle in comparison, she was sure.

'This isn't easy to tell you, Marion.' Libby sat up straight in the chair with her hands together in her lap, as if attending a formal job interview.

'But we discussed it and decided that you ought to know,' added Fiona.

'Hmm,' so they were getting the girls to tell her. Whatever it was it must be bad.

'Carry on.'

'It's about Val's friend, Gary Jamieson,' Fiona again. 'He's not what he appears to be.'

'Can you please stop pussyfooting around and just tell me what's going on.'

'Gary Jamieson is trafficking young girls to sell as sex slaves and is also a murderer... I mean very probably a murderer,' Jim corrected himself and they all waited for Marion's reaction.

'How do you know this?'

It wasn't what they'd expected and they looked at her assuming that the information hadn't sunk in.

'Mum, did you hear what Jim said?'

'I did and did you hear what I said? How do you know this?'

'Tony was surfing on the Internet and as usual, listening to stuff he shouldn't have been. He intercepted some police business and heard them mention my mother's name and yours too so... that's how we found out.' Libby's voice trailed away and there was an unexpected gust of wind, which made them all look around the room and a knowing look passed between the twins.

Not very likely, thought Marion. 'Show me the website.'

'I can't do that, Mum. They must have realised that someone was hacking it and it's been encrypted, but not before we discovered that the police are following that guy.'

'Who did he murder?'

'Err, don't know,' said Jim.

'Well you said he's a murderer. How do you know that?'

'The police said they suspected him of murder and child trafficking,' said Tony and Marion noticed how relieved his brother looked at this explanation. She let it go for now and waited for them to start questioning her. She didn't have long to wait.

'You don't seem very surprised,' said Fiona. 'I know you don't like the man but I expected a stronger reaction.'

'I already knew,' that shut them up. 'I've just returned from the People Against Poverty headquarters and have been informed that Gary Jamieson and Daniel Mulenga are being investigated on suspicion of trafficking young girls to sell as sex slaves. Three girls disappeared from our orphanage you see.'

'And my mother still wants to see this man?'

'Aah.' Marion studied her hands.

'She doesn't know does she?' Libby got up to leave the room.

'Libby, come back please,' Marion rushed to her and put her arm around her, supporting her to her seat as if she were an invalid.

'They've made me promise not to tell your mother, Libby. Although she already knows that Daniel is under investigation. If I do tell her and Val doesn't believe me the lives of many young girls could be at risk. Your mother's like a sister to me and you'll never know how much I care for her, but...' Marion put her head in her hands and shook it. 'I know it's going to be the death knoll for our friendship but I can't have the lives of God knows how many young girls on my conscience.'

'I hate not telling her as well.'

'You haven't told her? I'm surprised. I would have thought that...'

'Mum. We wanted to speak to you about it first and then we were going to tell her.'

A likely story. Marion could see that Tony was lying again and she wondered why they couldn't or wouldn't tell her the truth. The story about hacking the police website was so obviously a lie. Who were they protecting she wondered. Maybe it was someone close to Gary who was grassing him up – she thought that's what they called it - and maybe they'd given their word not to say anything. That seemed unlikely too, so why weren't they telling her the whole story? Knowing the twins as she did there was no point in trying to get the information out of them. They could be as stubborn as their father when the mood took them. Well, she could be pretty difficult too and Sylvia had told her that she wasn't to tell anyone about the police tracking Val's emails and phone calls. It might be too much of a secret for Libby to keep.

Tony noticed his mother's lips turn downward and a frown appear in the centre of her forehead and wondered where her train of thought was taking her.

'Mum, Mum!'

She looked up. 'Right. As there's a police investigation I don't think you should tell your mother, Libby. We have to protect her safety, right?'

Libby knew that Marion was right. Her mother was smitten and she knew that even if she tried to tell her about this awful man, her mother wouldn't believe her, especially the story about how they got hold of the information. And there was no way she could tell her about Tony's sister. She would also know that they had been talking to Marion behind her back, so it was a lose, lose situation. Libby knew that even with the outcome of Gary Jamieson being caught by the police, her mother would still feel wounded and betrayed by them all and have a broken heart as well.

*****

Claire and Raphael had watched the whole proceedings and although she was initially angry with

132

her brothers for going against her wishes, she had still nearly collapsed with laughter when Libby was explaining to her mother how they found out about Gary Jamieson. Raphael had to hold her and put a hand over her mouth so that she didn't cause any further disturbances down there. She felt better when they discovered what Marion already knew and was pleased that her mother hadn't been told that Gary and Big Ed were one and the same.

'Come on, let's go home,' said Raphael and he had that look about him that she already recognised and that meant they'd have some fun when they were back in Cherussola. Claire was so grateful for Raphael. Jay had been the love of her life and she never thought she'd experience lovemaking again. Death was getting better than it was cracked up to be and she knew she'd be with Raphael until one of them was sent to heaven for eternity. Claire knew that this wouldn't be for a long time, she didn't know how she knew, but was absolutely certain that Cherussola was her home for the foreseeable future. Perhaps it was something to do with her ever-increasing powers but she wasn't going to dwell on that at the moment. She looked at Raphael and took hold of him. He could travel much faster than her and she knew that she was in for one heck of a ride, or possibly two she laughed as they shot through the universe like the Enterprise on Warp Factor 10.

*****

Val and Marion met at the coffee shop by Victoria Station again to walk to the HQ and start their pre-deployment training. They hadn't seen each other for almost two weeks and Val looked tired and drained.

'How are you?'

'I haven't heard from Gary. I'm worried about him.'

133

Oh heck. Marion knew Val would think her false if she expressed concern for him and callous if she didn't – a no win situation.

'I'm sorry to hear that, Val. Can you contact anyone else?'

'You're not sorry at all are you?'

Marion didn't want an argument within seconds of meeting her nor did she want one in public. 'You know how I feel, Val but you must also know that I'm concerned about you.'

'I'm sorry, Marion. It's just that I'm tired. He's probably not in a Wi-Fi zone so can't FaceTime me. It's still worrying though.'

'I'm sure he'll be fine. He's a capable and versatile man and he managed to get to forty something without your help,' she gave Val a gentle nudge and they both laughed.

'Yeah, you're right. Come on, let's get cracking. I wonder who's taking the training?'

'Gail.'

'How do you know that? The letter didn't say.'

'She told me when you were in the loo after that meeting. I just forgot to mention it, that's all,' Marion couldn't see a reason why Val would check that with Gail so hoped she'd got away with the lie.

They walked on in silence, Marion worrying about Val and Val worrying about Gary.

*****

Val and Marion were staying overnight in the hotel and Jim and Fiona had invited Tony and Libby for dinner

It was Tony and not Libby who picked up on the atmosphere as soon as they arrived at his former flat, though it wasn't long before Libby sensed that something was going on. While the hosts were in the small kitchen Libby nudged Tony.

'What's going on? It's like they're hiding a big secret or something.'

'Act normal and don't say anything,' said Tony, wanting their hosts to crack first.

Fiona entered the lounge and he gave Libby a warning look. She handed Libby a glass of white wine.

'Nice glass,' Libby lifted it to the light and swirled the wine around. 'Is it new?'

'Engagement present, took them out of the box earlier. Thought we'd get the good stuff out tonight.'

'And very nice they are too.'

Fiona looked from one to the other. 'Beer, Tone?'

'Please.'

'They're not biting at all,' Fiona said quietly when she was back in the kitchen. 'It's not natural.'

'We'll drop a few more hints during the starter, they're bound to be curious then.'

Fiona nodded and Jim followed her with their drinks as she took Tony's beer through to the lounge.

They spoke about Val and Marion for a while, expressing their concern about Val's involvement with Big Ed, and hoping that the police would arrest and charge him before the women returned from Romania in a few months.

'They're back at the end of October,' said Jim. Fiona looked smug when Jim imparted this knowledge but Tony just said *oh really* and Libby looked down without saying a word.

Their behaviour was unnatural thought Fiona who decided to try a different tack.

'I wonder what the weather's like in Spain in November?' she asked.

'Oh it's lovely,' said Libby. 'I've been there in the late Autumn and it got up to the low twenties during the day but it can be chilly at night,' she had fond memories of her girls' break and started regaling them with stories of what they'd all got up to. 'Of course that was a few years ago now, but I don't think it will have changed much…'

'Sounds great. Do you want to go to the table and I'll bring the starters. Give me a hand, Jim.'

'We're having starters?'

'Yes, Tony. Well it is a special night.' Fiona's tone of voice indicated that she felt it was anything but special. She was surprised when Tony and Libby burst into fits of laughter and, like Margot out of the Good Life, failed to get the joke.

They put her out of her misery as soon as the laughter was spent.

'Do you want to tell us what's going on now or during dinner?'

'Actually, I don't know what you mean.' They weren't getting it all their own way.

'Sorry, Fi but it looked like you were fit to burst. And you, Jim. What's going on?' Libby put a friendly arm around Fiona and gave her a squeeze. 'Come on then. How do you know when Mum and Marion are coming home on leave and what's the Spain connection?' as Libby asked the question Jim walked to Fiona's side and they held hands. Either expecting or getting married thought Libby, and knowing how Fiona felt about her career, she guessed which one.

'Is it safe to say you're getting married in Spain in November then?' Tony got up and hugged his brother and future sister-in-law.

'Well done, Sherlock,' said Jim as Tony and Libby congratulated them both.

'There is more actually. But I think we'll keep that until the main course.' Fiona was determined to have the last laugh as she disappeared into the kitchen.

Curious to discover the rest of the news, Tony and Libby rushed through the salmon starter wondering what was coming next.

Libby helped Fiona take the plates to the kitchen while Jim recharged the glasses. The plates loaded with steak and chips, Fiona sat down with the eyes of Tony and Libby boring into her.

'Right. Help yourselves to the salad, please,' she pointed to the bowl and it was Jim's turn to be amused now. He avoided his brother's eyes.

'Enough, Fi,' Libby put down her cutlery and leaned forward. 'You've made your point. Now what is it?'

A look passed between Jim and Fiona and he spoke. 'We wondered if you wanted your blessing to take place after our wedding ceremony?'

'And we thought it was a cracking idea so we've arranged it,' added Fiona. 'But I can easily cancel it if we've been too presumptuous…'

'What a brilliant idea, thanks guys,' Tony looked to Libby. 'What do you reckon, Lib?'

Libby was wiping tears from her eyes and nodding her head. 'This is going to put things right between Mum and me and your family will be there already so that's not a problem. I'll have to make sure I can get time off work. Plenty of time to get a dress and there'll only be a dozen or so people who we'll have to invite separately and…'

'Whoa,' said Fiona. 'I've made a list.' She passed Libby a piece of paper full of names, some with ticks and some with question marks at their sides. 'We thought you might have twenty or so people you may want to invite that we might not know about. It's not going to be that big and we were planning on having a big party for the ones who can't come and the not so close friends and family when we get back off our honeymoon. Can I take it that's a yes?'

'Yes, yes, most definitely yes!' Libby was laughing now and Tony was well happy. He could show off the woman he loved to his close family and friends and also be a big part in his brother's special day. He wondered if he could be a groom and best man on the same day. As usual, Jim's thoughts were in tune with his own.

'You'll still be my best man of course?'

'But of course.'

'Your father's going to be there too.'

'I would hope he'd be invited, Fi.'

'I don't mean that, Tone. He's already going to be there. There's some big competition he's in…'

'European weightlifting championships,' added Jim. 'He's getting really serious about this and damn good as well.'

The rest of the night consisted of wedding talk and both Tony and Jim were glad when the evening came to an end. There was no doubt that they loved their ladies, but wedding planning wasn't their favourite pastime.

They agreed that they'd give the good news to Marion and Val before seeing them off at the airport later that week.

'Bit of good news for them to take with them and something else for Val to think about rather than that awful man.

'How did you find out about their leave,' asked Tony. 'They'll only be away for just over two months. They usually don't have a break until at least the three month point.'

'I phoned the charity and they put me through to the trainer,' said Fiona looking smug again. 'The woman's name was Gail and when I told her what the plan was she sounded nearly as excited as I was. Apparently she's quite close to both your mothers and thought it was a fantastic idea.'

Fiona went on to explain that the first phase of the Romanian deployment was helping with the light stuff in respect of the building of the orphanage, and getting things ready for the orphans who were currently in dilapidated accommodation that should have been condemned years before. They'll move them in on phase two, take a bit of leave, then go back and run the place for a while leaving the duo who are currently there to start a new project elsewhere.

Despite recent developments in their relationships and the worry about Val's friendship with a fugitive from justice, the twins and Libby were inordinately proud of their mothers. It was remarkable how the ladies had turned around their lives since the death of Val's husband and Marion's daughter, and also the disintegration of her marriage.

Before Tony and Libby left, Fiona and Libby told the twins that they would take a long weekend to Spain to meet the coordinator and to ensure the venue was as beautiful as Fiona said it looked on the Internet.

The date set, the couples said their goodnights, the women looking forward to carrying out the planning during the next few months and the men looking forward to the actual day.

Chapter 12

Even though they'd bribed some of the officials they were told that the girls still had to be hidden.

'The customs deputy is a Christian with a large family who he dotes on,' said Captain Saul.

'But I thought my money was used to bribe the Chief?'

'It was, but the man is bloody minded enough to risk losing his job by putting me away. On top of that his wife is championing the cause against child sex and slavery. She's even got her own website and Facebook page, damn woman.'

'You have Facebook here?'

Captain Saul gave him a strange look. 'We're not all tribesmen who live in the bushes you know. The 21st century has arrived in Africa.'

Gary hadn't witnessed much of the 21st century on this continent where the usual laws of life and death seemed savage, even by his warped standards.

'We sail tonight at 11 pm. The ship gets inspected at 9 or as near as dammit. That means that we will need to put the girls in the last container that's loaded. I've already told the customs that we're expecting a late delivery. They'll inspect it, I'll get it into the crate and the girls will get in before it's loaded. As soon as we sail I'll get them out of there.'

'What cargo are you carrying?'

'Scrap metal, cheap sweatshop clothes and handbags.'

Gary raised his eyebrows and Captain Saul smirked. 'Times are tough, Gary. If that indeed is your real name? I take the business where I can get it.'

'Don't ask stupid fucking questions, Saul, or I'll take *my* business elsewhere,' he emphasised the my and Saul acknowledged the comment by holding his hand out to shake. Gary accepted the gesture; no more would be said about his identity.

'Now, is there such a thing as a decent computer shop here? I need something a bit specialised.' Gary explained his needs.

'I told you we're civilised. You can buy just about anything you need here. I know a reliable source. I'll make a call to see if he has what you want and one of my men can take you,' Captain Saul smiled his most disarming. 'Don't barter with him. He knows to give you the best price or I'll kill him and his fucking wife.'

So much for them not being savages thought Gary. 'Thanks. Will he be able to deliver it to Europe and can I trust him to do so?'

The captain nodded.

Arrangements were made and shortly after a dusty indiscriminate vehicle pulled up. Gary raised his eyebrows.

'Too flashy and we draw attention from unwanted sources.'

Fair enough he thought. 'I'll be back to board the ship at 8.30 ish. And, Saul, be careful with the cargo, they're worth a lot,' he was about to get into the back of the car and turned to face the captain. 'Especially the girl Mary, she's very talented and I don't want to hear that anyone's messed about with her.'

'Don't worry, my men like real women and just in case they were tempted, Daniel's already put them in the picture,' the captain leaned into the car with a serious expression on his face. 'You may want to see a doctor while you're in town and get him to check you over.'

Gary was pleasantly surprised to hear the comment about Daniel but the pleasure turned to annoyance on hearing the captain's final remark. He must actually look as bad as he felt. He decided to ignore the comment.

'Move it,' Gary gave the driver a rough poke in the back and the man looked to his captain who nodded. The car pulled off with Captain Saul making a mental note not to share anything with Gary or the girl Mary, that would put him at risk of catching whatever it was. He suspected the worst and would also tell his men to ensure they knew the score.

*****

While Gary was away Captain Saul set about getting the ship ready to sail. The scrap metal had already been loaded and so had the first four of the five containers carrying cheap clothes and handbags made by women and children who hadn't heard the phrase *minimum wage* - they just wanted enough to be able to eat each day.

The final delivery arrived and the dockworkers set about filling the last container. The girls were sitting nervously in the small room where they'd been kept since their arrival. There were two potties in the corner which they'd been told to use, the only time any of them had been outside the room had been to accompany one of the crew when they went to empty their waste. They'd been fed and watered and didn't want for anything – like farm animals thought Mary, remembering better times. They knew they were to be smuggled onto the boat and the captain's men had seemed to become more nervous and tense when checking on them as the day wore on. The door opened and the small man entered. A few bottles of water were passed around for the girls to have a final drink; there was enough for them to have no more than a sip each. He pointed to the potties and told them all to use them and that he'd be back in ten minutes when it was time to leave. Mary rightly assumed that they wouldn't be

142

able to relieve themselves for a while. The door closed behind the little man and she could see her fear reflected in the faces of the other girls. Knowing they didn't have any choice but to follow instructions she used a potty and the other girls quickly followed suit. He returned shortly after with two other men and told them to follow him. It was dark outside and it took a few seconds for their eyes to adjust from the stark light of the bulb in the room. Although they were frightened, it was good to get outside into the air and there was a slight breeze coming off the water, which freshened their skin and made them all feel slightly cleaner. The walk was far too short and when they arrived at the container the small man whispered to his colleagues.

'In you get, girls and quickly.'

They looked up at the green metal box. The doors at the back were open and it was full of crates, most closed except the ones the girls were directed to climb into.

Mary looked around at the other 27 girls, 23 who had travelled with her from Zambia and the newly arrived 4 who looked more terrified than the others. She wondered if they'd been kidnapped from their families or if like the rest of them, they were already orphaned. The men lifted their shirts and pulled out small guns and the girls realised they didn't have any choice but to follow their orders. This wasn't a surprise to the older ones who'd become used to doing exactly as they were told. Two of the new ones started crying and many others followed suit, terrified of dying in the big green box. The small man took a step toward one of the crying girls and slapped her with the back of his hand. The shock of the slap stunned her and took her breath away and she stopped crying, froze and looked at him, like a rabbit stuck in the headlights of an oncoming car.

'Shut up and get into the container. Find an open box and jump into it, two in each box. Come on now and if I hear another sound out of any of you, my men will rape you and throw you into the sea when they've finished. Nobody will know and you'll be fish food.'

Mary knew they were valuable cargo and it was unlikely that would happen, but she also knew that the boss seemed to be able to get girls from wherever he wanted so the loss of one or two of them might only be a minor inconvenience to him. The man's words did the trick and slowly the girls walked into the container, quietly, one by one, resigned to whatever fate had in store for them. The last girl muttered to herself and started crying, despite what the scary man had said. Mary looked at the small youngster who couldn't have been much more than nine years old. She couldn't understand what she said but could tell from her gestures that she didn't want to get into a box on her own. Mary pushed Tamara toward her and told her to share with the little girl and to offer her comfort. She got into a box on her own and started to pray. Eventually they were sealed into their boxes and the container was closed. Even though it had a ventilation hole, the heat was unbearable and the air thick and humid. Tamara held the girl she shared the box with and whispered to her, hoping she would calm down because her sobbing was making it difficult for her to breathe, and the more she cried the more she panicked. The loud noise from above silenced the girl. Her tears were replaced with trembles when they felt the container being lifted.

The driver stopped outside what looked to Gary like one in a row of shacks. He turned to face his passenger. 'We're here boss. I'll wait here for you.'

Getting out of the car and walking towards the building Gary could see various items on display. A tall skinny man opened the door before Gary got to it and his smile lit up his black face. He put out his hand for Gary to shake and nodded his head in a small bow-like gesture. 'I'm John, sir. At your service and to cater for your every need.'

Gary wanted a computer and nothing else and he impatiently explained this to the man. Bowing again, the smarmy John asked him to follow and took him through to a small back room. Despite Gary's explanation he clapped his hands and two women appeared through a door at the back of the room. John sat back in his chair looking smug and told him to take his pick. Gary refused the offer and John unsuccessfully tried to hide his surprise. Gary told him he was in a hurry and wanted to get down to business and John fired up the laptop on the desk in front on him. He opened a website containing images not fit for any eyes except those of the most depraved people alive. Gary tried to hide his disgust and explained that the laptop was for a friend and that it should be encrypted so that messages to and from it could not be intercepted. From the look on John's face he wasn't convinced his words were getting through to the man. He leaned forward and further explained that there should be no shortcuts pre-loaded to illicit website addresses or anything else of an offensive nature emphasising again that the laptop was to be the property of a decent friend. In case there was any doubt, Gary added that if he later discovered his instructions had been disobeyed, he would hunt him down and remove his testicles with a chainsaw before burning his eyes out and killing him. As he looked into his eyes John knew that he would rather be thrown into a sea full of sharks than face the wrath of the white man in front of him. Business concluded, Gary left the shop satisfied with his purchase and that his instructions would be followed.

*****

Those that had them were told to bring their own laptops for the training.

'Ooh that's nice. I haven't seen that before. Did you treat yourself?' Val opened the lid on her new laptop and Gail remembered the last course that Val was on when she said she'd need to use one of the charity's computers because hers was so old.

Marion could see that Val looked like the cat that got the cream so pretended not to listen and definitely didn't want any part in the conversation, guessing where the computer had come from.

'It's a gift from Gary, arrived this morning. I didn't want to accept it but it's hard to refuse when something's sent to you in the post, isn't it? He's so kind and obviously very keen to keep in touch.'

Yet again Marion wanted to vomit.

'Very kind of him,' said Gail with as much enthusiasm as she could muster, but both women could tell she wasn't being sincere.

As with anything related to Gary, Val was blind to anybody else's feelings and always thought something else was going on. She went for a comfort break and mentioned it to Marion when they were next on their own.

'Do you think we should push it to see what's wrong with Gail? Her reaction to my good news was so out of character and I'm quite worried about her.'

'It's the stress from work, Val. Like all charities People Against Poverty are struggling. Gail was telling me they'd had to sack a lot of the admin staff so they have to arrange their own travel, overnight stays, type

146

up their own reports etc…all stuff that she used to have done for her.'

Made sense to Val and she could understand why Gail didn't seem as bubbly as she'd always been.

'She's probably overtired as well as stressed out. Shall we offer to help?'

'No!' Marion's protest was over the top and Val leaned back in surprise.

'Sorry. You know how independent she is, she'd be mortified.'

'Fair enough, Marion. Good job nobody else was about, you would have frightened the life out of them.' Val had a feeling that something funny was going on but couldn't quite put her finger on what. She'd have plenty of time to think during the nights in Romania, although her previous experience had shown her that after a full day's work, her body told her brain to shut down and very often she was too tired to think. Sometimes that was the best way to find a solution as the harder she thought about something the more elusive it became.

'We'll see,' said Val more to herself than anyone else.

Marion gave her a funny look but deigned not to comment.

The break over and the training continued. Despite Gail's skills both women were in their own worlds and would have to read the hand out from the session to find out what the lecture had been about.

The two days of training and familiarisation flew by and Val and Marion said goodbye to Gail following dinner on the second day.

'Take care, both of you and we'll see you in a few months.' It was the most serious that either woman had seen Gail and they said their goodbyes and made their way back to the station.

'Gail was a bit over the top wasn't she?' Val asked while they were waiting to cross the road. She was too busy watching for a break in traffic to see the fleeting expression on Marion's face.

'I expect she was thinking about that business in Zambia and hoping there wouldn't be any surprises this tour.'

'Maybe you're right. Funny how that Daniel disappeared before they had a chance to question him though... come on, looks like it's going to tip down,' Val grabbed Marion and they rushed across the road as the first raindrops started to fall from the grey sky that was slowly turning black. Marion was amazed that Val was totally blind to the link between Daniel and Gary, which seemed glaringly obvious to her. It wasn't very often that she was grateful to the good old British weather that had put paid, for the time being anyway, to any further conversation about Gail, the events in Zambia and those horrible men.

Both wanting to get home and sort their gear out for Romania, they agreed not to delay their journey further with coffee or tea and to meet at the airport three days later.

'We can always phone if we want to pick each other's brains,' said Val. 'I still think Gail's attitude was out of character though.'

'Ah well, maybe she's got other stuff on her mind. When's your train due?'

The diversionary tactic worked and they said their goodbyes and went their separate ways.

*****

Back at the docks Gary showed his papers to the official and made his way to the ship. They sailed 30 minutes after the expected time, which meant the girls had been in the container for over 3 hours. Captain Saul said they'd need to get out into the open sea before opening the container and bringing out the

148

girls, and he assured Gary and Daniel that there would be no adverse effects of their 4 hours or so in the claustrophobic box.

As they opened the container doors a little while later and the girls filed out gulping in great breaths of sea air, they heard the sound of an engine in the distance.

Captain Saul laid a hand on his employer's shoulder. 'Here's our insurance.'

They watched as the large speedboat pulled alongside the freighter and Gary viewed from the higher deck as one of the crew threw a ladder over the side from a lower deck and six men climbed the ladder and jumped onto the ship. A rope was then lowered and one of the remaining passengers secured a box, which was pulled up and onto the ship.

'Munitions,' said the captain, stating the obvious.

This was repeated a further three times. The passenger then looked up and saluted and the captain called his thanks before the speedboat disappeared. The latest arrivals appeared on the deck and if looks were anything to go by, Gary was impressed. Had he not hired these six mercenaries he would have been extremely wary if confronted by any of them, and he was the meanest and most dangerous man he knew. Gary laughed to himself, so far so good. Captain Saul had fulfilled all his requirements and could find himself a regular employee of Gary in the future. Saul told Gary that he'd tell the men who the boss was but Gary wouldn't be able to talk to them directly as they didn't speak English. Happy with that Gary didn't want any new friends, just confidence that any attacks by potential pirates would be met with savagery that brooked no forgiveness and no repeat offenders.

*****

For this farewell they'd decided to meet in the city for breakfast before Val and Marion departed for the airport.

They'd discussed whether dinner and a night at the theatre might be a more appropriate time to break the news but had decided against it. They'd already had a get together with a family dinner and night out a few days before Val and Marion started their training, and Val was delighted that Carl and his new girlfriend had been able to attend.

Jim called his mother to make the arrangements. 'We have news,' was all that he had said, under strict instructions not to let his mother wheedle any additional information out of him. Libby had told her mother that there was something they all needed to discuss. Carl couldn't make it to the breakfast but his sister had already told him the plan and he'd been all for it, confirming enthusiastically that he'd definitely be at the wedding. Val and Marion discussed both calls and rightly assumed that an actual date had been set for Jim and Fiona's wedding. They managed to work out that the blessing would take place round about the same time but having experienced the major disappointment of Libby and Tony's secret wedding, neither woman wanted to build up her hopes too much, just in case their assumptions were incorrect.

The café was around the corner from the charity headquarters and also convenient for Victoria Station where Val and Marion could go directly after breakfast to catch their train to the airport.

The tea, coffee and orange had been served and the youngsters were asking Val and Marion about Romania while waiting for their cooked breakfasts to arrive. The older women waited patiently until Jim nodded to Fiona. Clever, thought Marion. Fiona was the only non-blood relative and the twins knew that if their mother or Val wasn't happy with the news, they'd be less likely to have a go at her. The betrothed couples hadn't even considered this. Fiona being the most forthright had volunteered to break the good news and the other three had agreed.

'You may be wondering why we asked you here today?' she raised her voice to ensure she had their full attention and there was a smile playing on her lips.

'As you probably suspected, we've set a date.'

Marion clapped and Val smiled.

'What you might not have suspected is that we're getting married in Spain.'

'Oh goody,' said Marion, but Val waited in anticipation of news about the blessing.

'And…' she looked at Libby who took the hint.

'…And we're going to have our blessing after Jim and Fiona's wedding. We've booked the venue and Fiona and I are going out for a long weekend in September to make the final arrangements.'

The mothers were delighted and they discussed the date and venue. Val hoped they'd have enough leave for her to be able to see Gary at the same time, but kept that thought to herself.

Marion noticed the twins looking at each other. There's more she thought. When nothing was forthcoming she prompted. 'Is there something else you want to tell me?'

This time they had planned for Fiona to give Marion the news. 'We've invited Graham, Carol and Mel, Marion. I hope you don't mind?'

Val stopped thinking about Gary when she saw the look on Marion's face. She waited for the fireworks, but none arrived.

Yes she did bloody mind, she minded very much. She should have anticipated this and knowing what young Mel had been through, and she still couldn't bear to think of the girl as the twins' stepsister, she didn't have a choice. She tried to adjust her features so they couldn't see how bitter she still felt about the whole affair. So much had happened since Claire's death and the end of her marriage that she should be over their bastard father by now, despite his deceit of nearly two decades.

'Not a problem. I'm sure the hotel will be big enough for us to be able to avoid each other,' although Marion's smile was false, they decided to ignore it and all breathed a collective sigh of relief.

They said their goodbyes knowing that the next time they saw each other would be in Spain, prior to the wedding and the blessing. Not overweight but a little heavier than she wanted to be Marion vowed to lose 7 pounds by the time they went to Spain, adamant that she would look her absolute best when she met up with her ex-husband.

Val tried to switch off on the journey to the airport and hoped that Marion would have it all out of her system by the time they boarded the aircraft. They were flying to Baia Mare in the north of the country. With the one stop off the flight time was approximately seven hours. The new orphanage site was about 90 kilometres away from the airport in Sighetu but all that was much too long to be listening to Marion's comments about her ex-husband and his family. On the flip side, Marion probably didn't want to hear her talking about Gary. After they checked in Val looked tentatively at Marion and put a hand on her arm to get her full attention.

'Can we do a deal?'

Marion pre-empted the next comment.

'I know, I know. Okay. I'll shut up about that bastard Graham if you don't talk about,' she hesitated, not feeling brave enough to say what she thought. Val got her drift and interrupted.

'Gary. I won't talk about Gary. Well not to you anyway.'

They laughed as they made their way to the departure gate. Sometimes the old magic of their friendship was still there.

*****

It was the happiest Mary had been since she'd been taken from the orphanage. Despite the fear of being suffocated in the container they'd all survived though some of them had got through the experience with fewer scars than others. Mary looked at Frea, the young girl who had followed her around since they'd left the container what now seemed like ages before. They'd stopped once to take on more cargo and supplies and now they were in the middle of the ocean again. Even if they'd wanted to escape there was nowhere to go. Consequently they were left more or less to their own devices. The boss had used her on that first night and he'd been particularly rough, but since then none of them had seen much of him. She'd seen him eat once and his face had turned a funny colour and then he'd run to the side of the ship and vomited into the sea. Mary wondered if he had the disease on him or if it was nothing to do with her. She looked up, glad that her parents had returned and were helping her again. She thanked them for making the boss ill and also for whatever they had done to stop the other men from molesting her and the other girls. It had been a while since she had something to thank anybody for and the fresh sea air and a full stomach was enough for now.

Gary tentatively got up from the bed in his cabin. The only time he felt reasonably human was when lying down. The sickness returned as soon as he stood up and he fought to stop it rising to the surface. He looked down at his emaciated body and wondered when he would next be able to eat a meal without it making an appearance a few minutes later. He had never felt so weak and was seriously worried about his health and strength. Weakness was an anathema to him and despite his timeframe to meet the businessmen in Algiers, he considered where they could stop off for a few days in order for him to regain his strength.

Gary sent a hasty email to Val. He didn't mention his illness, not wanting her to think any less of him. He was able to tell her of the progress the ship had made and how he'd lucked out by buying and arranging to sell the shipful of scrap metal. In her previous email she'd asked whether he'd known that Daniel was being investigated. Gary feigned surprise in his response and told Val that he hadn't seen his former friend since her and Marion had left. From the tone of her last and previous emails, he had no doubt that she'd believed him. He closed the computer hurriedly when he'd finished and rushed to the heads. There wasn't much in his stomach and he'd been sick so many times that it hurt with the latest bout of retching. He decided to have a sleep and if he felt better when he woke up, would summon Saul and discuss another possible stop off with him. As he lay down with his arms tight around his stomach trying to stop the pain, he wondered if this was what hell was like. He wouldn't have too much longer to find out.

The noise woke Gary and it sounded as if all hell had broke loose on the open deck. By the time he dragged himself out of his bed and took his rifle out of the cupboard, it sounded as if trespassers had boarded the ship. Pirates he assumed and he couldn't work out whether his mercenaries or the invaders were winning the battle. He heard girls screaming and his sense of urgency doubled – not because of a sense of gallantry, but because he would lose money if the uninvited visitors kidnapped any of his girls.

The man that grabbed Frea's arm was over six foot tall and stank of rum and corruption. Mary didn't notice as she acted without thinking. Putting her hands around the smaller girl's waist she pulled as hard as she could. The pirate had been told not to harm the merchandise but this one was slowing him down and irritating him like a small yappy dog.

Mary's interference bought them the time they needed and Captain Saul seemed to appear out of nowhere, fury and murder in his eyes. He swung the machete and the last thing that Mary saw was the look of shock in the pirate's eyes before his head dropped to the deck with a dull thud, the eyes still open and staring at both girls. His hand still held Frea's arm for a few seconds after his head was separated from his body. The attack ended as suddenly as it had begun and had it not been for Frea's high-pitched terrified screams, the ship would have been absolutely silent.

Even feeling like death, Gary had still managed to kill two of the pirates and their bodies soon disappeared into the unforgiving sea, along with all the others. The crew and girls watched for a few seconds as the sea seemed unnaturally calm and silent. Suddenly the water churned and a feeding frenzy started, sharks and smaller fish devouring the bodies and minutes later all trace of the pirates had disappeared.

Captain Saul said something to one of the mercenaries and a rope ladder was thrown over the side of the ship. Before the leader descended the ladder, he gave one of his team the evil eye, punched him in the face and said something to him. Gary didn't need to speak the language to work out that the punched guy was the one who must have slept during his watch, his lethargy almost causing disaster for the ship, her crew and passengers. His lack of action proved how ill he was – had he been in rude health, the man would have been fed to the fish along with the marauding pirates. He summoned Captain Saul while watching the head mercenary board the pirate vessel that had been tied to the freighter. The captain explained that he'd given the man orders to salvage anything of value from the ship and to untie it and set it on fire as a warning to any others in the area. He also explained that the inattentive mercenary would be led to believe that his punishment was the punch and a loss of pay but would be dealt with appropriately once ashore. They might need him relatively healthy until then and it was unlikely that he'd fail in his duties again. The attack had decided Gary that he would bear the sickness until their arrival at Algiers rather than risk a diversion and another possible invasion. He returned to his cabin without even asking what the real punishment for the useless mercenary would be.

The memory of the head hitting the deck played over and over in Mary's mind. She felt no sympathy for the pirate, only gratitude for the captain and something else. She'd told herself since her kidnap from the orphanage that she had to look out for herself and trust no one. Her guard had lapsed and she'd allowed Captain Saul's kindness to get under her skin. She trusted him like no one else since her family had died and her gut told her that he would look out for her. She cursed her feelings but no matter how much she argued with herself, it all came down to her instinct and she hoped that she wasn't in for another disappointment.

Chapter 13

Marion and Val had started work as soon as their feet hit the ground at the orphanage building project. They'd been there almost a month and were about to have their second day off. They'd done some sightseeing during their first free day. Having been told that conditions in some of the orphanages were still dire, despite major improvements since the fall of the Communist government in the latter stage of the previous century, they knew that a number of charities were working very hard to improve conditions but were keen to look around and see for themselves. They did not pre-warn the management of the two orphanages they visited in the countryside. Whilst facilities at the first were adequate, the second caused major concern. There appeared to be a lack of medicines and the washing facilities were dirty and inadequate. Some of the children were bruised and both women suspected physical abuse at the very least. Many of the children were uncomfortable around the staff and when one of the female staff went to stroke the head of a little girl, Marion had the distinct impression that it was just for show. This was confirmed later when a young boy cowered as if he were about to be hit. By the time they returned to their modest accommodation next to the new build they were both very upset and agreed that they should file a report to *People Against Poverty* without delay, with a suggestion that their charity combine with two others and take over the running of the establishment as soon as possible. It amazed them both that children were treated like they would have been in an eighteenth century workhouse, yet less than 100 miles away lots of money had been spent to provide an internet connection. Though grateful for this facility it was a very distressing dichotomy.

Val said she'd type up the report – her typing skills were better than Marion's and her new laptop was much more modern. Having completed the report Marion stood behind so that both women could scan it for errors, prior to sending it to Sylvia at the headquarters. Before they'd finished the machine pinged indicating a new email. Impatient to read it in case it was from Gary, Val minimised the report without checking to see if Marion had finished reading.

'Oi. Do you mind?'

'Sorry, Marion but I'm hoping for news,' she hadn't heard from him for a few days and was excited. She certainly hoped it wasn't some stupid Spam message telling her that she'd inherited millions of dollars from a dead relative she didn't know she had.

'Okay. I'll just go for a pee. Can we get that report in soon though, so they can act on it quickly?'

Val bristled. She only wanted to check her bloody email for God's sake and would take seconds. Marion read her body language and didn't wait around for her reply. By the time she returned from the toilet Val looked as if she'd won the lottery.

'Good news?'

'Yup. It's just nice to hear from him and to know he's all right. Let's get this report off.'

Val told Marion the barest details of every email she received from Gary. This suited Marion who would be more than happy not to hear any further news about Gary, ever. Although, if Val did want to share anything with her in future she would feign interest but only for the sake of their friendship.

When Marion checked her own messages later that night, she was surprised to see one from Gail marked urgent. She assumed it was related to the report, but once she'd opened it and started to read, she was glad that she hadn't called Val prematurely.

Elbows on the makeshift desk and palms holding her cheeks, she stared at the words trying to make sense of the request and wondering what she should do.

The gist was that the police had been unable to decipher the emails being sent to and from Val. They assumed that some sort of sophisticated encryption had been employed and needed Marion's help to get information about Gary. So from being totally disinterested Marion now had to pretend she gave a damn. Val wasn't stupid and would know she was faking interest and she emailed Gail to explain the problem. Gail had suggested that Marion eat humble pie and tell Val that she might have been wrong about Gary. She ended the email with: *do what you can, but remember, this man sells children for sex.* So, if she didn't help and he evaded capture the lives of many girls could be ruined. Nothing like a generous dose of guilt to spur on this particular call to action. Thought Marion.

*****

A week to go before docking in Algiers and Captain Saul was in a dilemma. The girl Mary had followed him around whenever she could since the pirate attack and that meant that the small one, Frea was also on his trail. Missing his own kids who'd long since grown up he'd shown them the workings of the ship and taught them about fish in the local areas. Mary hadn't shown the slightest sign of illness and he'd revised his initial assumption about her condition and enjoyed her company. He'd explained the ship's position by showing them a map. Mary had been fascinated so he'd also shown them the globe and explained where they were going. She was like a sponge and had taken in everything, asking intelligent questions and even beginning to laugh and joke with

159

him. Frea had not said a word but became very distressed if Mary wanted to go somewhere without her. She even had to accompany her to the toilet and wait outside. Mary showed maturity beyond her years and had seen too much in her short life. Saul suddenly realised that he couldn't let the girls go to the life that Gary had planned for them. He would keep the two girls and give them the life they deserved – a risky strategy, but Gary may be too weak to push it and if he insisted then... Saul tried to put his finger on when his feelings had changed and concluded that it must have been when Frea had slipped under the deck railing and looked as if she were going over board. As usual, Mary was there in a nano-second and had grabbed Frea's leg. Both girls would have slid over the wet deck had Saul not saved them and he'd felt more than relief when Mary had put her arms around his neck and hugged him tightly. He remembered how close he'd been to his kids and missed this closeness now that they were grown up and gone on to better lives. He'd decided there and then that Mary was going to be his granddaughter and therefore by default, so would Frea.

*****

Ron and Sandy had been following Val and Marion. Ron knew that Val was planning to meet Gary, but hadn't been able to read her emails and was frustrated that he couldn't work out where and when. They watched as Marion attempted to garner some information.

'I'm really looking forward to the wedding. Only a week. The last couple of months have flown by.'

'Hmm,' Val looked up from her book and smiled at Marion. 'I'm so excited. Libby's emailed me a photo of her dress, it's so beautiful. She's going to look stunning.'

'Fiona's sent me pics of hers too. She's so thoughtful knowing how I'll never see...'

She didn't finish the sentence and Val put her book down and gave Marion a hug. She couldn't imagine what life would be like without Libby and her heart went out to her friend. They talked about the dresses and other wedding details for a while. Then Marion thought she'd try again to get the information that Gail required. She had so far been unsuccessful.

'What are you planning after the wedding?' her attempt to look genuine and interested didn't fool Val and the question drew a wedge right through the good feelings of moments before. Both women knew Val was going to see Gary.

'Oh, you know. A bit of this and that. Thought I might do the touristy thing for a few weeks before we return here. And you?'

'No plans as yet. Fancy some company?' 15 all thought Marion.

'Umm. Well actually, Marion, my plans might change at short notice and it'll do us good to have a break from each other. So if you don't mind I'll say no. Are you all right with that?' Game set and match to Val although Marion could see that she was genuinely concerned that she hadn't hurt her feelings. Her stomach churned. She was no good at this cloak and dagger stuff and the stress was making her feel ill. Val was right in that it would do them both good to have a break from each other, which they always did between tours and when on leave. And now Val thought that she might be hurting her feelings by turning her down. She decided to come straight out with it.

'You're absolutely right of course about us having a break from each other,' Marion didn't make eye contact when asking her next question. 'Are you planning on seeing Gary?' There, it was out.

'I might. But there again I might not. Why the interest in Gary all of a sudden?' it seemed to Val that Marion had been fishing for information on Gary's whereabouts. She tried to remember when her curious questioning had started and thought it was about a month earlier. It had been amusing at first but was starting to get on her nerves now. She knew that her friend still couldn't stand him despite pretending otherwise. Libby had also taken a keen interest in her mother's future love life, which had been a little more awkward. Gary had told her that his agency was involved in the investigation of Daniel. He wasn't supposed to divulge any information to anyone but knew that he could trust Val with his life, if it came to it, and that she wouldn't share what he told her with anyone. Val knew they'd understand when the truth finally came out, but for now she wasn't going to betray his trust. She'd therefore told Libby that she didn't have any plans to meet Gary after the wedding, but would tell her she'd changed her mind, after seeing him. Hopefully her daughter would be too consumed with her blessing and the holiday after – she'd refused to call it a honeymoon as they were already married, but that's what it was to all intents and purposes.

*****

When Gabriella arrived at Cherussola Raphael was trying to field a number of quick-fire questions from Claire. The whoosh only stopped her momentarily and Gabriella decided it was time for more to be revealed. 'You've probably already worked out that some angels on Earth are born to normal families.'

She hadn't, but kept quiet in the hope that further information would follow. Gabriella didn't disappoint.

'They are already old souls and their parents know they're special from a very young age,' she checked to ensure that Claire was still listening, knowing that she very often had a short attention span. 'Saying that, all parents think their offspring are special and friends and relatives often miss the signs. To a lot of people there are few things more tedious than parents talking incessantly about their own *brilliant* children, and our special children know not to show off from quite a young age.'

Seeing Claire's stance with the folded arms and a sceptical look that she'd been unable to mask, Gabriella could see she'd given her more credit than she deserved. It would probably come as a shock but the time was right.

'You have to remember that these may be young children, but they're still old souls, emotionally mature beyond their years. We start visiting them when they're very young and they don't fear us. When they talk to their families about the visits, parents smile and humour them, knowing that it's perfectly normal for young children to have imaginary friends. By the time they reach their teenage years, they know they're angels and that they've got a job to do. They move amongst ordinary people doing good deeds and stopping evils from carrying out their heinous acts, where they can. They know the basic workings of the universe and that they've been sent to love and protect humans. This isn't a problem as we love naturally. What is sometimes an issue is that we love too much and that's how some humans have special qualities that occasionally take us by surprise.'

Having seen Ralph, Claire wasn't surprised to hear that angels walked amongst humans on Earth. She was trying to get her head around the other information and Raphael could see that her brain was working overtime. It looked for a moment as if everything had clicked then Claire looked confused again. Raphael went to speak but Gabriella put a hand on his shoulder. 'Let's see if she can work it out.'

'So I must be descended from an angel. There's no way my father's an angel, well I hope not, anyway?'

Raphael and Gabriella's eyes told her that her assumption was correct.

'My mother's grown as a human but I can't really see her as an angel?'

'Correct,' said Gabriella. 'I'm going to put you out of your misery, Claire. This happened a while ago. Generations can be skipped and all of a sudden, someone can have the traits or talents of an ancestor and we have to do the research to discover who it was and when it happened.

'Similar to human genetics then?'

'Exactly.'

So she really was special. They'd seen the same reaction on many faces before and both knew it wouldn't be long before the expression would be wiped off by the enormity of the responsibility she faced.

'I hate to rain on your parade, Claire, but it was merely chance. An ancestor of yours and an angel fell for each other and didn't think about the consequences. Unlike the evils who mostly plan their issue. Look where that leaves us.' They all looked down.

Claire saw a woman lying naked on a bed no detail had been spared as she looked on in horror at the large man pounding away at her. His flesh rippled in blubbery waves with every thrust and the act that she only knew as an expression of love or pleasure, looked like an obscene cartoon porn show. Although she appeared to be uncomfortable, the woman lifted her hand to look at her watch then lifted her eyes to study the ceiling, obviously bored. When the man glanced at her she bit her bottom lip and squealed before calling unconvincingly *yeah, baby, yeah.* The man didn't seem to notice she was faking and Claire would have laughed had the image not been so dismal. The scene disappeared as quickly as it had arrived and Claire was suddenly viewing a building with long corridors. A buzzer went off somewhere in the distance and a cacophony of sound accompanied many young children as they headed for their classrooms. A little girl, younger than eight Claire guessed, headed for the girls toilets and a boy followed her at a distance. Claire only saw the back of the girl but she could see the little boy clearly and with his shoulder-length blond hair hanging in corkscrew curls and baby blue eyes, he looked like a little angel at first glance. When she looked closer she noticed the expression on the boy's face and cringed. His mouth was smiling but the boy's eyes didn't match it. Claire could see the malice and knew he was up to no good. It was as if a camera had panned to another scene and they watched as a teacher asked his pupils to be quiet. He looked around the class.

'Where's Angelo?' no answer.

'And Elfie?' a little girl raised her hand. 'Yes, Phoebe?'

'Elfie's got a funny tummy, sir. She had to go to the toilet.'

Mr Graham didn't like the sound of Angelo being missing at the same time as Elfie. The school had already discussed his bullying with his mother to no avail. The Head had therefore taken the step of writing to the woman and threatening expulsion. The next step would be to involve the local authorities if the child's behaviour didn't improve quickly. Mr Graham knew who and what Angelo was. One of his jobs was to stop the child from harming others until he was eventually claimed by his own. He knew this might last into adulthood and Mr Graham might be replaced by another at any time. Until then he'd do his job to the best of his ability.

'Open your books at page thirty seven and draw a picture of the bird in the story. I'll be back in a few minutes.'

Mr Graham went to the classroom next door and the teacher agreed to keep an eye on his class until his return. He hurried along the corridor to the girls' toilets and pushed the door – nothing happened.

Claire looked at Gabriella and Raphael in confusion and Gabriella gestured that she should keep quiet and watch.

He could hear little Elfie screaming inside, but no matter how hard he pushed, the swing door wouldn't budge. Knowing that Angelo was being assisted, Mr Graham looked upwards and said one word.

'Help.'

He felt a change in the atmosphere and the door started to move, slowly, as if a tug of war was taking place between those who wanted it closed and those trying to open it. It seemed like an age before the door was open enough for him to squeeze through but was in fact a matter of seconds. He rushed inside and stopped in front of the sinks. Elfie's hands were tied around a water pipe at the other end of the sinks, she was trembling, sobbing and shouting for her mother. Angelo had a knife in his hand and had already hacked away at Elfie's clothes, which were hanging off her in tatters. The child was terrified as the boy had a tight hold of her ponytail with one hand, smiling as he was about to cut into it with the other hand that held the knife. Mr Graham could see he was getting pleasure from torturing the little girl. Knowing how evil the child was, he didn't need to wonder how far he would have gone, had he not arrived to stop him. Mr Graham bounded over to the children in record time and grabbed Angelo by his knife arm, stopping him from chopping Elfie's ponytail. He lifted him off the ground by the same arm and the knife clattered to the floor. Angelo's face spewed pure rage and he kicked and punched at the grown man with all of his might. Elfie watched in fear, her sobs turning to shudders.

'I'll be back in a minute, Elfie. You're a brave little girl,' shouted Mr Graham as he tried to get a firmer hold on Angelo in order to avoid his punches and kicks. The stream of abuse was horrendous and he switched off to it, not trying to communicate with or placate the little boy. He didn't have any trouble with the swing door on the way out and Mr Graham was grateful that the host had prevailed. He almost collided with the Deputy Head who had hastened toward the toilet as fast as her short legs would carry her when she heard the screaming and shouting coming from inside.

Her eyebrows asked the question.

'Angelo has been torturing Elfie Dixon, Mrs Foster. Would you please untie Elfie and comfort her, she's tied to a pipe in there,' he gestured with his head trying all the time to control Angelo who was apoplectic with rage. The Deputy did as asked and Mr Graham carried the boy along the corridor. The scene disappeared.

'So Angelo is the result of an evil sleeping with the prostitute?'

'That's right.'

What was the outcome of his behaviour?'

'Claire, this was merely to show you that we're not the only ones with a presence on Earth. Ours is a constant battle against evil. If they prevail...'

The smug expression had long disappeared from Claire's face as she contemplated her role in future fights against evil.

By the time Ron and Sandy returned to Cherussola, Raphael had comforted her and Claire was back to her normal self. She could see that they were disappointed that they hadn't been able to provide the information that Gabriella had requested.

Ron hadn't seen Claire for what felt like ages and he noticed the change in her. She appeared taller and her grey eyes seemed to have a permanent sparkle. He realised that the impression of additional height was just a deception. He watched as Claire and Raphael whispered to each other and laughed, all the while touching and oblivious to the presence of the other three. She was more confident and obviously in love thought Ron. He was happy for her, thinking back to the night of their death over two years before and the occasional pang of guilt he still felt for cutting her earthly life short on the night her fiancé had proposed. Last time he'd seen her, Claire had told him that her fiancé Jay had set a date for his wedding and she hadn't seemed to mind at all. Although it made him feel better that she'd found love again, he was a little jealous that he would never have another physical relationship. He thought that he and Sandy may have feelings for each other but Gabriella explained that only a chosen few on this side could progress to that sort of relationship. There was no spark between them but they were good friends and would always be unless given different paths to take. Whilst he knew that he would go to heaven eventually, and so would Sandy, Claire's future was to take a completely different route. Gabriella had told her that heaven would be her soul's final resting place but her *special abilities* would be put to good use before then. As usual Claire had pressed for further information, knowing deep down that none would be forthcoming from the beautiful angel. He was unaware of the information Gabriella had shared with Claire and the former's voice, chastising the loved-up couple, stopped his daydreaming.

'Hello. Remember us?'

Raphael whispered to Claire before looking at his sister. Claire put a hand over her mouth and giggled like a naughty schoolgirl and Gabriella raised her eyes upward. She gave them a few more seconds to calm down and clapped her hands. Claire sat up at the sound and gave Gabriella her full attention. Ron hid a smirk and they all waited for the angel to speak.

'Through no fault of their own Ron and Sandy have been unable to discover the whereabouts of Gary, or where he's arranged to meet Val. We have some work to do.' Gabriella explained that she'd been given the go ahead from the Committee to withdraw many spirits from their current duties.

'Gary needs to be followed and we need to know where he's arranged to meet Val. I don't want to risk anything until we have the back up sorted. We know they're going to meet sometime after the wedding so when I give the go ahead I want you guys to hang around the wedding party. We'll find the enemy as soon as I've made the necessary arrangements.'

She didn't need to tell Raphael not to attempt to find Gary until they had the support needed, he was well aware of the risks. But looking at the others Gabriella knew they each had a reason for wanting him stopped, and would likely take undue risks to do so. She'd need to chat to Raphael about it in private.

'Raphael, the Committee want a word with us both. It won't take long,' she turned to the others. 'Wait here until Raphael's return please.'

Charming. Thought Claire. Although Gabriella had said please, it had not been a request.

Raphael looked at his sister and wondered why she was lying to him. He also wondered why he still allowed her to boss him around, despite him having been a member of the Committee and technically senior to Gabriella. On the first matter, he'd find out soon enough, he thought as he followed her towards her home and not to the Committee Chambers, the second would take more time to figure out.

'I'm worried about the confrontation,' she hesitated and Raphael waited for her to gather her thoughts. 'They seem to think we're infallible and despite Claire's near hell experience, if you and I are around I just know that the three of them will take too many risks.'

'Keep them in Cherussola?' Raphael knew it wasn't really an option but was at a loss as to what else could be done.

'Ron and Sandy, possibly. The trouble is Claire can now come and go as she pleases without checking with me first...'

'She doesn't know yet,' interrupted Raphael and they both laughed, wondering when she'd discover her new capability.

"They've all been affected by his actions and in the interests of fairness they should all be allowed to have a part in his downfall.'

Gabriella's thoughts mirrored her brother's words and they contemplated the best way forward. When they next locked eyes, the twins knew that they'd come up with a potential solution at the same time.

'So we are going to see the Committee then?' Raphael took his sister's hand and they made their way, unannounced, to the Chambers.

*****

After almost nine weeks of constant travelling Captain Saul told Gary that this would be their final night on the ship and they would dock early the following evening. In order to avoid the ships that constantly surveyed the area, checking for smuggled goods and people, they'd had to take a circuitous route and their journey had therefore taken longer than Gary had expected. After Val had emailed him her plans he'd asked the captain to dock at Oran instead of Algiers and Saul had agreed to make the change, but this had also delayed the journey by a few days by the time he'd received the approval from the port authorities and arranged for his legal cargo to be disbursed. He hoped that Val would appreciate his sacrifice; every moment he was on a moving ship was absolute hell. Gary had also had to arrange for his buyers to meet him in Oran instead of Algiers. He wasn't worried about messing them about. He'd sent them an email saying he'd had reports of a crackdown by the port police in Algiers and they'd readily, but nervously he sensed, agreed to meet him Oran. He knew that the chances of them backing out of the deal was about the same as him being sainted and they'd actually thanked him for the warning. Children were the paedophile's drug and they could do without them no more than an alcoholic could do without booze.

In Gary's cabin Saul knew that the time was now or never to tell him he was keeping Mary and Frea. Saul thought it would be easier to handle Gary due to his sickness but watching the man now he knew he'd made a major error of judgement. Looking into his eyes he had the look of a wounded animal about him and Saul knew that animals were most dangerous when injured. There was no way he could tell him that he was keeping the two girls. He toyed with the idea of asking to buy them but knew he'd have nowhere near the money that the European businessmen could afford and Gary wouldn't accept less, especially for his own particular star Mary. He'd have to think of something else.

'Did you hear me, Saul?'

Saul shook himself. 'Sorry, what was that?'

Gary had noticed a flicker of something in the captain's eyes but couldn't put his finger on it. He knew he wasn't stupid enough to deceive him but also knew enough not to trust anyone in this business.

'I said have you sorted the bribe and does the cargo need to go in the container again?'

'Yes to both. And I've booked you in to see a local doctor as soon as we dock. He's got a good reputation.'

Gary was grateful for that, the captain seemed to have good contacts wherever they went. He wasn't going to be distracted though, never mind how ill he felt and he'd arranged to meet his two purchasers the following day.

'I want to see the girls being loaded into the container and when they leave it. If it means them staying in there a bit longer while I see the doctor, so be it.'

'Don't you trust me?' Saul hoped he hadn't sensed his weakness. He took his knife out of the sheath and held it up to the light. He looked at Gary and ran the blade along his own thumb, drawing blood. He wiped the blade on his trousers, sucked the wound until the blood flow stemmed and returned the knife to the sheath.

The gestures weren't lost on Gary who lifted down his rifle and inspected the weapon. He cocked it and loaded a cartridge before laying it on his bed. 'Of course I trust you, Saul, but I'm not sure of the others, even Daniel. Business is business, my friend,' he patted Saul's shoulder reassuringly and the captain could feel the weakness in Gary's body.

He knew he could easily kill this man dispose of his body and more than likely get away with it. All the men on board would back him except Daniel who could be dealt with in a similar manner. Saul had already thought this through and one of the differences between him and Gary was that he had a conscience. Saul would only kill if his life or the life of others was in immediate danger, and he knew he wouldn't be able to live with himself if he murdered this man to save the girls. He would save the girls though and he had less than 24 hours to come up with a suitable plan.

As it happened, fate played a hand in his decision.

*****

The hotel had its own private beaches. Walking from the private entrance the setting was idyllic. White poles had been covered in white netting rolled up so that guests could see the plants and the sea in front. The white wooden chairs were bedecked with ribbons and flowers and a white carpet placed from the exit to the gazebo where the ceremonies would take place. Fiona and Libby looked at the setting in awe while the twins looked at their wife and fiancée, simply pleased that they were happy. The party were getting together for a quiet dinner later and that was of more concern than the actual ceremony. Marion and Graham would meet for the first time since she threw him out of the marital home and the twins hoped that they could put their differences aside for the sake of the wedding and blessing. Looking out to sea, Jim put his arm around Fiona and gave her an affectionate kiss on the cheek.

'Fantastic. I can't believe you've arranged all this without anyone to help.'

Despite her capabilities, Fiona loved it when he heaped praise upon her and she couldn't have been happier. 'Glad you like it.'

'Like it, Fi? I love it. You've got a real talent for this you know,' he pulled her close and gave her a long kiss. 'Clever girl.'

She could see the twinkle in his eyes and holding hands they ran back to the room Fiona was sharing with Libby until after the ceremonies. Giggling at each other because Libby and Tony were out sightseeing and they'd be able to make the most of the few hours before dinner with all the family.

*****

Marion's stomach was in knots. She was to come face to face with the woman who'd been having an affair with her ex-husband for more than 16 years of their marriage and would also meet their daughter. She didn't want to get into it with her and planned to say hello, but very little else. She'd discussed it briefly with Val earlier and Val said it was only natural to be nervous and apprehensive. She'd added that Marion would also feel curious, angry and probably a whole range of other emotions that would be perfectly normal under the circumstances. Val had then disappeared for the afternoon and told them all that she'd meet them at the restaurant later. But Val had been wrong. Marion had been through a gamut of emotions when her suspicions had been confirmed that Graham had cheated. She'd let go of the anger slowly following Claire's death and although she'd never forgive Graham for making a large part of their marriage a lie, she didn't feel any love for him or jealously about the other woman. She did however feel nervous, curious about Carol and her daughter and uncomfortable about the forthcoming meeting.

Approaching the venue with the twins and the girls, Marion acknowledged to herself that her life with Graham was now history and she wouldn't fret about the past. Despite this, she felt as tense as a coiled spring, and was shaking inside. She tried to act as normal as possible but evidently this hadn't worked. The twins were walking ahead and Marion had picked-up on the look that Fiona gave Libby.

'Tony, hang on a minute,' called Libby. 'I just need to check...' her words petered out as she turned to

174

Marion and Fiona and shrugged her shoulders then jogged to catch up with the twins.

Fiona put an arm around Marion's shoulder and couldn't hide her surprise at the tenseness in her future mother-in-law's body. 'You don't have to go you know. If you're not up to it you can do something else, and I'll come with you.'

It was a lovely gesture and Marion was so pleased that Fiona was going to be part of her family. Despite her feelings, her ego wouldn't let her miss this dinner, and anyway, they were meeting Fiona's parents, Nigel and Linda, at the restaurant and Linda would be very unhappy if she dragged Fiona off elsewhere. Marion reminded herself of the image in the mirror prior to leaving the hotel room. Her hair was newly styled and coloured for the wedding and even the twins had been complimentary about it, telling her she looked younger and actually meaning it. She'd reached her target weight and her stomach was the flattest it had been since having three children almost three decades ago. For someone who had never been confident with the way she looked during her entire life, now in her early fifties Marion was at last happy with her appearance, where she was in her life, and the excitement of an unknown future. Her shoulders relaxed and she smiled at Fiona and reached across and patted the hand that was around her shoulder.

'I'm fine, Fi, and I wouldn't miss this for the world.'

Fiona felt the stiffness leave her and knew that Marion meant every word of it. She gave her a squeeze and a smile and they walked the rest of the way chatting about the events of the following day.

The inside of the restaurant was on the strip and the outside opened onto the beach. Diners could choose whether they wanted to eat outside or in and they'd decided to eat inside, as the autumn breeze could feel cool once the sun had gone down. Val arrived from the opposite direction as the twins and Libby arrived and they said their hellos before going into the restaurant and meeting Graham, Carol, Mel and Fiona's parents.

Marion and Fiona arrived shortly after, arms linked and in animated conversation. To any onlookers it appeared that neither had a care in the world.

'Your ex-wife,' said Carol from her seat at the bar as she looked at the happy go lucky woman entering the restaurant with Fiona. The woman looked nothing like the stern individual that Graham had shown her a photo of years before. Graham could hear the incredulity in Carol's voice and he wasn't surprised. Marion looked years younger than she had when they were together and something about her made her attractive to men of a certain age. It wasn't her looks, which were average except for her intelligent blue eyes which took in her surroundings in a matter of seconds, maybe it was her air of confidence and the impression was of a woman who was entirely happy in her own skin. Or it could have been the fact that Marion wasn't aware that she was attractive to the opposite sex, that was always appealing, thought Graham. Her eyes now landed on him and he noticed the flicker of surprise with satisfaction, before she was able to hide her feelings. He had an unexpected tremor in his gut and tried to make sure it didn't show on his face.

'Ow!' Graham reacted to the elbow in his side and looked at Carol.

'Remember me?' she asked.

Despite the ups and downs of their relationship, they'd recently decided to give it another go and the newer, more sensitive Graham sensed his partner's insecurity. He turned her head toward his and kissed her full on the lips. Mel cringed with embarrassment and Marion thought that thumping his fists on his chest might have been less obvious. She took in his new improved physique and reminded herself that it was still the same deceitful bastard under the newly formed muscles, as she walked confidently toward the bar accompanied by Fiona with a smile stuck on her face.

Chapter 14

After his chat with Gary the captain had called for the leader of the mercenaries to come to his cabin. He explained his plan and asked the man if he wanted to earn extra money. He knew he couldn't trust him, but also knew that he could be bought by the highest bidder. The mercenary had seen Captain Saul behead the pirate and knew that if he took his money and deceived him afterwards, he could expect a similar punishment. He wasn't surprised when the captain had told him he was keeping the two girls. Anyone who'd seen their relationship develop during the weeks on board would be aware of the fondness and the bond that had been forged. The only one not aware was Gary as he'd spent the majority of the time in his cabin.

'Daniel could be a problem,' said the mercenary. 'Shall I talk to him?'

Christ knows what that *talk* would involve thought Saul as he shook his head. 'After you search the ship and inform me publicly that you've found nothing, all he'll have is suspicions that he'll be able to report to his master. He may even be too frightened to tell him if he has no proof. Whereas if we warn him off...'

He let the words sink in and the mercenary nodded in understanding, gaining a new respect for the man he'd previously assumed was mostly brawn.

After dismissing the mercenary Saul spent some time wondering what to tell the girls. He knew that Mary was close to the one they called Tamara and might not be able to resist saying goodbye to her. Best if it was a surprise to all of them. He called a trusted member of his crew and explained his plan.

Tamara opened her eyes. It was very dark so it must have been a noise that had woken her. She couldn't see a thing but neither could she sense anything wrong. She thought she'd felt a presence in the room and listened intently. The only thing she heard was the breathing of the other sleeping girls and she convinced herself that a dream had awoken her. She closed her eyes. They all knew that the following day the ship would arrive in port and it was probably worrying about what her future held that had woken her. Lying with her eyes closed all seemed well on the ship and she soon drifted back off to sleep.

Mary and Freya both tried to wriggle out of the grasp they were being held in. But each man had a tight hold on each girl's body with one hand while their other hands were clamped respectively around each girl's mouth. Mary stopped wriggling, trying to work out where they were. They appeared to be heading to the captain's cabin and she knew that he wouldn't hurt either of them. She calmed down and tried not to let her wildest hopes and dreams form as coherent thoughts. Frea looked at her, wide-eyed and terrified. Mary winked and saw the younger girl visibly relax. She knew if her friend and mentor wasn't frightened, she had no need to be.

Arriving at the captain's cabin the door opened and the men entered.

'Shhh,' said Captain Saul as the men put down the girls but kept their mouths covered. He put a finger to his lips and nodded to emphasise the point.

'Okay?' he asked and the girls nodded back. 'Nobody's going to hurt you so be quiet and listen carefully.'

They nodded again and so did the captain, but this time to his men. The men relaxed their hold on the girls and then released them completely. Mary opened her mouth to ask a question but Captain Saul whispered for her to be quiet.

'You are not going ashore with the other girls tomorrow, you are coming with me.' He smiled slowly and Mary put a hand over her mouth, stopping herself from voicing her delight when he'd just told them to be quiet. She hugged herself and then opened her mouth again. The delight quickly vanished from her face and the others in the room could see that she was trying to work things out, as if the news was too good to be true.

'Quietly,' said the captain as he hunkered down. 'Freya walked into his circle as if it were the most natural thing for her to do and they both looked at Mary.

'Have you bought us?'

He assumed her concern was because she thought he might sell her to someone else. He was disappointed that she may think that of him, but could understand after what she'd been through.

'No. You're coming with me and your boss will think you've jumped overboard. I have to hide you and you both have to be very quiet until I can get you off the ship. Do you understand?'

'What are you going to do with us?'

'I'm going to take you home and you're going to be our granddaughters.'

He held out his arms and Mary ran into them, her quiet sobs ones of joy and relief.

*****

Fiona pretended to listen to her mother's chatter as she watched the introductions. She thought that Marion and Carol sized each other up like two animals about to go into battle. They shook hands. 'How do you do?' said Marion and Carol inclined her head and smiled falsely without repeating the greeting.

'This is my daughter Mel.'

Marion wasn't hostile toward Mel. Acknowledging the fact that her parents' indiscretions weren't her fault.

'Pleased to meet you, Mel,' the warmth in Marion's voice was genuine. 'The twins have told me loads about you and you do have Claire's eyes. Look at this photo.' Marion took the photo of Claire out of her bag and Mel studied it. Her stepbrothers had told her about her likenesses to Claire before but she'd only seen group photos, which hadn't been particularly clear. This one was a head and shoulders shot of Claire in school uniform, at a similar age to what Mel was now.

'Oh, her hair's lovely. I wish I had curly hair,' she hesitated, feeling slightly uncomfortable. 'I'm so sorry for your loss, it must be awful for you.'

Marion appreciated that and said that yes, it had been and still was pretty awful even though Claire had been gone for over two years. The moment passed and she brought the conversation back to hair, telling Mel that Claire's curls had annoyed her daughter. They discussed the fact that most women with straight hair preferred curls and vice versa. Carol looked on quietly, miffed by the fact that her daughter was getting along so well with her partner's ex. She wanted desperately to dislike the real Marion as much as the one she'd imagined her to be, but was finding it difficult so far.

Graham was almost forgotten about whilst the women discussed the plans for the following day. He breathed a sigh of relief and watched as Fiona manoeuvred the conversation, ensuring they stayed on safe ground and keeping Carol and Marion away from each other. Val was happy to chat to Carol and tried to get inside her head so she could report back to Marion later on. Graham caught the eyes of his sons and they ostensibly made their way to the gents, but quietly stepped outside the restaurant.

'That went better than expected.'

They could see that the earlier tension had left him and their father was now relaxed. They'd come to terms with what he'd done to their family and learnt to live with it, but since Graham's breakdown they were concerned at how he'd react in emotionally charged situations. Despite his new size and strength, they knew he could be overly sensitive and prone to emotional relapse so had been watching intently, ready to intervene during any difficult conversations if required.

'I'm all right, really.' Graham felt more like the child than the parent but was glad to have his two strapping lads looking out for him. He had to admit that it was down to Marion and not him that they were able to talk about their feelings without getting embarrassed, something that had taken him a long time to achieve and he still wasn't particularly comfortable doing so.

A round of manly arm punches ensued and the three made their way back into the restaurant. The twins entirely comfortable now that their parents were settled and able to concentrate on their next task, garnering as much information from Val as they could.

*****

Gary awoke to loud voices on the final morning of the journey. He could hear Saul shouting but there was no panic in his voice, just anger. He took a drink of water and sat down for a few minutes to ensure it wasn't going to come back up. Feeling weak he dressed as quickly as he could and made his way up to the deck to see what the problem was.

As Gary was on his way up Captain Saul was making his way down to his cabin and they met on an unmanned deck.

'The guard who messed up on duty has disappeared.'

'What do you mean *disappeared*?'

'Exactly what I say, Gary. Their leader woke me earlier and told me he's missing. They're searching the whole ship now, along with my crew to see if he's hiding.'

Gary held his chin with his thumb and stroked it thoughtfully with his index finger. 'Anyone or anything else...'

He stopped talking and they both looked up as they heard footsteps rushing down the stairs. Daniel appeared, breathless, and immediately behind him was the leader of the mercenaries.

'Two girls are missing.' Daniel didn't wait for the invitation to speak. 'Mary and her little sheep.'

'Shit,' said Gary and the captain tried his best to look surprised. He spoke to the mercenary leader then turned to Gary.

'His man has definitely disappeared and he thinks he's taken the girls with him.'

'But how could he do that without sounding the alarm,' Gary felt his blood boil and it gave him strength. He covered the short distance to the mercenary and punched the man with all his force. The man hit the deck, banging his head on the stair as he did so. Blood spurted out but he was still very much conscious and had murder in his eyes. He regained his composure and sat up, his hand moving toward the knife in his waistband. Daniel moved toward him and grabbed his hand before it reached the knife. Gary moved to pounce on the man but Captain Saul took hold of him and stopped him before he could do so.

'Enough!' his voice stilled them all for a second. Had Gary been at his normal size and strength Captain Saul would not have been able to hold him back, but the anger had left him feeling tired again and the captain could feel him slump in his hold. He spoke to the mercenary in his own language and the man shook his hand out of Daniel's, pushing Daniel away at the same time. He put his hand on his head then looked at the blood on it. He said something to Gary who didn't need to know the language to understand the meaning.

'This will get us nowhere,' Captain Saul said to all of them, then turned to Gary. 'The others knew nothing about his disappearance. It seems pretty obvious that he's taken the girls.'

'I want compensation.'

So it was all about the money then, thought Saul. 'May I remind you that you employed these men and if you think you can get a refund from him,' he thumbed towards the man who was still sitting on the stair, 'then good luck with that. Be my guest.'

Gary knew he was the meanest bastard on the ship. But he also knew that he couldn't fight them all in his weakened state. He would put this one in the bag for another day, but return to it he would and get his revenge. He looked to Daniel who seemed to be about to say something.

'What is it?' that's all he needed, another fucking problem.

All eyes turned to Daniel. Saul was pleased to see that the expression on Gary's face had made him reconsider.

'Shall I get the other girls ready to leave.'

Gary nodded. 'Get rid of him too,' he said to Saul and the mercenary disappeared after a few words from the captain.

When they could no longer hear footsteps Gary stood up to his full height and leaned into Captain Saul's face, invading his space. 'I will not forget this and I will find out what really happened here.'

It took an iron will for Saul to look him in the eye. He could feel the evil emanating from the man and if he let this go without comment Gary might figure out the truth. Even though he was ill, Saul was convinced that he'd come back for him and he tried to force down the bile that was making its way to his throat before replying.

'You already know what really happened. I'm not making it up. Ask any of the men, any one of them.' The last words were emphasised and Gary stepped back and studied the captain. He was pleased to see that the man was frightened and that he could still terrorise powerful men, even in his present state of health. He spat in the captain's face and Saul quickly wiped it off his cheek, the veins in his neck sticking out as he did so.

Saul struggled with his emotions, his fists clenching in and out. He turned around swiftly and ran up the stairs without saying a word. He could kill the man now and knew his crew were loyal to him. But Gary would be off his ship within a matter of hours. He'd bank his money shortly after and would never have to see the bastard again. He hoped he had the illness and that it would soon lay waste to him. He also hoped that he had all the misfortune his enemies wished on him until his time ran out. Saul hurried to his cabin and scrubbed his face until he was satisfied that all traces of the saliva and potentially killer bacteria contained within it had disappeared. He knew the disease couldn't be transmitted in that way unless he had an open wound, but he was as superstitious as the next man. He had the girls and he had won so why then did he feel like a sad, dirty loser? Maybe it was time to turn legitimate and to say goodbye to Gary and his like for good.

*****

Carol was put out that Mel had asked to sit next to Marion at the dinner. As her eyes drifted to her daughter and her previously sworn enemy she could see they were still getting on like a house on fire, through the first and onto the main course. Graham was talking to Fiona and Carol used the lull in the conversation to look around. It seemed that she wasn't the only one who was miffed with her daughter. Libby had been leaning across the table talking to her mother and there was silence when Val raised her voice in response.

'Enough with the questions! I didn't realise that my love life or lack of it, was of such interest to you lot,' she pointed to Libby and the twins in turn. Fiona lowered her head and wasn't included.

'Mum!' Libby was embarrassed.

'Mum nothing. It's your big day tomorrow and all you and the twins seem interested in is when I'm going to see Gary. What's wrong with you all?'

'We have your best interests at heart, Val, that's all,' Tony winked at his mother-in-law. 'We're happy so we just want you to be too.'

Graham had taken a gulp of beer and he spluttered it over the table at hearing Tony's words.

'Dad,' complained Mel. 'Can't take you anywhere.'

'Bit OTT, son,' said Graham when everyone looked at him.

The conversation moved on but Graham noticed the look between the twins and Fiona and wondered what they were up to.

It was playing on Graham's mind when they returned to the hotel later that evening but when he'd tried to discuss it with Carol she wasn't interested. She was too absorbed by Mel and Marion's new friendship and bothered that Graham didn't feel the same way about it. He excused himself and put on his sports kit. Luckily the receptionist was a weightlifting fan and asked Graham for a signed photograph to which he obliged. The receptionist returned the favour and opened the gym for his hero. Graham always found his training therapeutic and he tried to piece together the events of the evening and come up with a logical explanation. He failed to do so but the more he thought the more he was convinced that his boys were up to something and that Val was somehow involved. By the time Graham had finished training he was exhausted but also determined to discover what was going on.

Marion had said goodnight when they returned to the hotel and made her way up to the room she shared with Val, who was having a last drink with Libby before retiring for the night. She took her clothes off and with them disappeared the enforced happy mood of earlier. She removed her make-up and cleaned her teeth, all the time thinking of the evening. She'd had a lovely time talking to Mel who'd turned out to be kind, pleasant and charming, no thanks to her parents, thought Marion. But it had also been a shock to look into those eyes and to recognise the familiar way she flicked back her hair. She'd also sounded exactly like Claire when she'd admonished Graham. Getting into bed Marion laughed at that thought and the laughter soon turned to tears. She still missed Claire so much, and knew she'd always miss her. As she approached that mysterious place between wakefulness and sleep, Marion heard her daughter's voice.

'I'm all right, Mum, I really am. I've met someone and I'm happy again. It's time for you to move on now and find someone to share your life with. By the way, you were brill tonight, Mum, really brill.'

Marion smiled to herself as she nodded off. Her baby was happy and pleased with her. All was well with the world.

As Claire left her mother she felt as she used to when work was about to finish on a Friday and she had the whole weekend to look forward to. She smirked to herself as she remembered once wishing she had a tail so she could thump it and everybody would see how happy she was. Those days were long gone but the uncertainties of death that she'd felt when she arrived at Cherussola with Ron were starting to disappear, and she was carving herself a place in this strange and mysterious world. Seeing her mother as a confident self-assured woman earlier had made her happy and so had her peaceful sleeping face just now, but Claire knew that the major source of her current euphoria was Raphael. Her wonderful angel who could take his pick of beautiful and intelligent beings had chosen to be with her. Claire hugged herself and decided to pop in and see how her father was getting on.

Graham looked at the chasm between him and Carol in the king-sized bed. She wasn't sleeping but was laying on her back with her hands behind her head looking up at the ceiling. She appeared to him to be deep in thought and had already told him that she wasn't happy about the way he'd looked at Marion earlier. He wondered if they were both happy to give their relationship a second chance as he tried to put Marion out of his head. It was only fair to think about Carol when he was with her and, he admitted to himself, the sex with Carol had always been fantastic. Sensing her eyes on him he didn't make eye contact but sat up in bed. She turned to him, elbow on the bed now leaning her head on her hand and looking at him intently. He could see she was curious out of the corner of his eye and he straightened his right arm and then bent it and flexed it so his biceps bulged, he did the same with the left, then winked at his lover.

'I'm almost impressed,' she said, a slow smile spreading across her face. 'But surely you can do better than that?'

They seemed happy enough to Claire but she sensed that something wasn't quite right with her father. Guessing what her father's performance was leading to, she had no desire to stay around and watch, so disappeared to see what her stepsister was up to.

Graham leapt off the bed and stood up straight. He flexed his arms in turn, making his pectoral muscles twitch and started humming a tune in rhythm to his muscle movements.

'Bravo, bravo,' shouted Carol and Graham continued to hum a tune as he stepped out of his boxers, his penis stood smartly erect.

'Come on then, Big Boy,' said Carol. 'Let's see how good you really are.'

Mel was in the bathroom and had just finished cleaning her teeth. She shivered and goose bumps suddenly appeared on her arms. She turned to look behind her very slowly and let out a big breath when she discovered nobody there. She tutted to herself and made her way to bed. Claire didn't want to scare her stepsister so left quietly and returned to the others.

*****

The guests were seated comfortably and waiting for the first bride to arrive. The music started and Marion turned around and gasped, not because of how wonderful Fiona looked as she walked down the aisle on her father's arm, but because Mel had had her hair curled and it could have been Claire that was following Fiona up the aisle, albeit a younger and taller Claire, but Claire nonetheless. Marion wiped away the first tear and tried her best to stem the flow of the others.

Claire also gasped at the younger and taller version of herself, even though she was still preoccupied with what had happened the previous night. She'd wanted to see how her mother coped with meeting

Carol but Gabriella hadn't returned and given her permission to leave. Frustrated, she attempted to move and had been surprised to discover that she could leave of her own volition. She had a lovely time watching them all at the dinner and had surprised herself yet again when she'd been able to pass the message to her mother. Whether or not her mother thought it a dream didn't really matter. Claire had noticed a new bounce in her step this morning and she was different somehow. Saying that, she hadn't seen her for a while and the difference might have happened previously without Claire noticing.

Jim and Fiona's wedding went like a dream and Claire was so absorbed in the proceedings that she didn't hear Ron and Sandy arrive. She jumped and a sudden breeze lifted one of the gazebo curtains. Fiona and Jim looked at each other knowingly and Marion smiled to herself.

Ron shook his head. 'You've got them all thinking they can sense you now you bloody Looney! What's Gabriella going to say.'

'Shhh,' Claire tried not to laugh or do anything that would cause objects to move. She still hadn't fully mastered her new talent and weddings made her too emotional to attempt to control those talents now. 'Let's just enjoy the ceremonies and talk about this later.'

Ron agreed, especially as the wedding ceremony concluded and the guests were enjoying a small break while Jim and Fiona signed the register. Libby and Tony's blessing would follow.

The ceremonies were followed by a lovely meal and some dancing to a live band in the evening. Marion was hot from too much dancing and an inconvenient flush so decided to wander outside into the cool breeze. Seeing Carol and Mel still absorbed in the music on the dance floor, Graham followed Marion onto the beach.

'Beautiful isn't it.'

She wasn't surprised to hear his voice as she'd seen him approaching the exit when she was leaving.

'It certainly is,' Marion kept it short, hoping he'd take a hint and leave her in peace.

'I miss our holidays.'

She looked at her ex-husband in amazement, wondering what planet he was currently occupying. 'Graham, when we were on holiday you were more than likely wishing you were with Carol.'

'Not all the time,' he drew a pattern in the sand with his foot and Marion knew him well enough to know he wanted something, but she wasn't sure what.

She wanted to be on her own and he was getting on her nerves. 'What do you want, Graham?'

'Do you think...' he stopped, struggling to find the right words and Marion had no idea what was coming next. 'Would you ever give me another chance?' he let out a long breath. There, it was out. He didn't expect her reaction.

Firstly, her mouth fell open of its own accord. Then the surprise turned to incredulity and she couldn't actually believe he was serious. Marion laughed hysterically. She knew her ex-husband wasn't the most intelligent man in the world, but for him to honestly think that she'd consider getting back together with him was hilarious. It was so funny that she was out of control and had to cross her legs so she didn't have an accident.

'I assume that's a definite no then?' he wasn't laughing and Marion nodded her head as vigorously as she could, still in hysterics.

'So this is where you got to,' Carol didn't like the scene in front of her eyes but tried not to show it. 'What's the joke?'

Graham looked to Marion to help him but calming down now, she decided to let her pig of an ex-husband get himself out of this particular pickle.

'We were just reminiscing about some of the antics the twins got up to when they were young and Marion was laughing about how they used to pull the wool over my eyes.'

'Must have been really funny,' said Carol looking at Marion for affirmation. None was forthcoming and she wondered what had really gone on.

'I'll leave you two to star gaze. Thanks for the laugh, Graham. I'm glad to see you haven't lost your sense of humour,' she returned to the party and Carol watched her chuckling away to herself until she disappeared through the door.

'What was all that about?'

'I honestly don't know.' Carol saw the bewildered look on her partner's face and believed him, though her gut told her that something had gone on but she had no idea what.

Claire watched her father make an idiot of himself and couldn't quite believe what she'd witnessed. She understood why he'd had a nervous breakdown after her death and the break-up of both of his relationships, but she still thought that deep down, he was an honest man. Claire thought that he'd fallen madly in love with Carol and that had made him deceitful but it was only now that the penny dropped and she realised that the man she'd loved and looked up to for years was actually weak, deceitful and dishonest. It didn't make her love him any less, but she certainly found it harder to like him. She would have been embarrassed had Ron and Sandy witnessed the scene with her parents and was grateful that they were watching the shenanigans inside.

The day had gone like a dream as far as Ron was concerned and he couldn't believe that he'd been lucky enough to attend both of his daughter's ceremonies. Ron had been over the moon when Claire told him later that Libby had asked Tony if her father had been at their blessing. Tony had replied that Claire had been so there was a good chance that he had too.

The guests had enjoyed themselves and the day was coming to an end. The happy couples retired to their respective honeymoon suites and Val had once again refused to divulge her plans for the rest of the holiday when Marion enquired.

Most of the guests were staying at the hotel the day following the wedding and intended to disperse the day after. Graham, Carol and Mel had booked another week so that he could compete in the European weight-lifting championship five days later. The newlyweds enjoyed a lie-in and leisurely breakfast then surfaced to swim, chill and socialise with their guests later in the day. They knew that Val was due to check out the following morning and prior to the ceremonies, the couples had agreed that the twins would follow Val and the girls would stay at the hotel and keep in touch by phone and email. Val's safety and the capture of Gary were paramount and neither couple thought twice about delaying their honeymoon. Oblivious to the fact that the twins were following her, Val made her way to the ferry booking office, excited that she'd see Gary the next day. In their turn, the twins were initially oblivious to the fact that their father was following them. Val exited the office and Jim followed her. Looking at the posters in the window Tony thought that the booking office was purely for ferries to and from Algeria. He tested this theory by asking the booking clerk on entering the shop. The woman spoke excellent English and confirmed his assumption. She also told him that the journey time was approximately 8 hours and the next ferry was due to leave at 9am the following day.

'It's very busy at this time of year,' said the sales rep lying through her teeth. 'I just sold the last ticket but let me see if I can squeeze you on.'

Tony gave her his most charming smile, grateful she'd given him the information about Val without him having to ask.

'I need two tickets actually, but if you're fully booked I'll have to look for an alternative...'

'Wait a minute,' she interrupted while tapping away at her keyboard. 'There appears to have been a cancellation.'

Yeah, right. He smiled again. 'I'll need a cabin as well please.'

The booking clerk's day was getting better by the minute and she chatted amiably while waiting for the tickets to print and for his credit card payment to go through.

As Tony left the office there was a furore outside and he glanced toward where the noise was coming from to see his father trying to draw attention away from himself. He was surrounded by a number of keen teenagers all pushing pens and notebooks at him. Tony could see that Graham was trying to keep them quiet but his attempts were having the opposite effect. When he saw Tony leaning against a tree with his arms folded and smirking at the scene, Graham gave up and graciously signed the autograph books. While the teenagers had his father's attention Tony phoned Jim. He told his brother about the tickets for the trip. Jim said that he was only a few minutes away and would meet him outside the shop, as Val was just sightseeing and shopping.

'You know that thing where women go into every open shop, look at every item and come out without buying anything.' Tony hung up feeling sorry for his brother. He'd been shopping with Libby and if her mother was half as bad, Jim had his total sympathy. Jim arrived shortly after and as the teenagers left, the twins approached their father.

'Nice day for a stroll, Dad.'

Graham ignored Tony's statement. 'What are you up to?'

'Don't know what you mean, Dad.'

'You were quizzing Val at the meal the other night. Now you're following her when you should be having fun with your new wives. What's going on?'

They knew there was no point lying to him, but they also knew they couldn't tell their father the truth.

'I'm really sorry, Dad, but we can't tell you,' Tony looked to his brother for support. 'You just have to trust us on this,' added Jim.

'I bloody knew it,' Graham clicked his fingers. 'You're some sort of special agents aren't you? What's she up to? Does Libby know?'

'Don't be ridiculous, Dad. Jesus. Talk about an over-active imagination,' Jim sighed.

'Are you taking something that's messing with your head?'

Graham studied his sons. So that's how they want to play it he thought, and understood that in their line of work they couldn't spill the beans.

'Okay, let's just forget I asked any questions. I'll see you later.'

'Do you fancy a quick drink, Dad?'

'No thanks, I'm going back to do some training. Catch you later.' He walked away hastily and left his sons looking at his disappearing back, dumfounded.

Jim and Tony decided to walk to the nearest coffee shop. They found a secluded corner and ordered their drinks, talking quietly about their strategy for the next few days.

As soon as he thought he'd be out of sight Graham turned. His sons were walking away from the booking agency and he doubled-back and entered the shop. The booking clerk was only too glad to confirm that a man had booked passage and a cabin for two passengers less than a half-hour before. Yes, she could definitely get him onto the same ferry and would print his ticket right away. How would he like to pay?

***

'Why do they all believe the special agent stuff?' said Claire and the others shrugged. Maybe it was a generational thing. Val and her father were quite close in age and perhaps people were easily taken in as they aged. She recalled the saying about the young knowing everything, the old believing everything and the middle-aged suspecting everything, but Val and her father weren't yet old enough to believe everything.

'They're too young to be that gullible. What's going on, Ron?'

This was a glimpse of the old Claire and not the new one with super-powers. Instead of Ron sighing and being exasperated at her questions like he would have been not so long ago, he was glad that she still needed him and occasionally found him useful.

'It's what they want to believe, Claire. Imagine the thrill for your father thinking that his boys are clever enough to be involved in that line of work. And as for Val,' he did sigh now. 'It's probably two-fold unfortunately,' getting into the swing of educating the two women Ron held his chin with his thumb and forefinger and adopted a thoughtful pose. 'Firstly, if she honestly believes that the man she calls Gary is really working undercover, this means that he simply cannot be guilty of anything her subconscious may suspect that he is. Secondly, her ego will be swollen with pride that a man so important could be mad about someone who

196

thinks of herself as an ordinary woman,' he smiled and nodded his head knowingly.

'You're so clever, Ron.'

Plainly he wasn't because he couldn't work out whether Claire was being sincere or taking the mickey.

'I want the twins to know that they'll have company tomorrow,' Claire quickly changed the subject as was her wont. 'Coming to the hotel?'

They were all nervous about what was next, both for themselves and their relatives and Claire thought watching the people they loved enjoying themselves might be a pleasant distraction, well for her and Ron anyway. Sandy didn't seem to have anyone to visit on Earth so was glad to go along with whatever Ron and Claire suggested.

After laying out the problem to the Committee Amanda told Gabriella and Raphael to wait outside while deliberations took place. Raphael knew it was his mother's way of showing her displeasure for his resignation and he sighed, wondering how long she was going to hold it against him. They didn't have long to wait before a Seraphim called them back in. They noticed that God had resumed his seat at the head of the Committee and his gentle but commanding voice echoed throughout the chamber telling them to take a seat. They did as bid and he spoke again.

'Your mother needs a change of scenery. She will accompany you prior, during and immediately after the mortal's death trip and I will assume my rightful place until I choose otherwise.'

So his mother who was still punishing him for asking to leave the Committee, wanted a break from it herself. The irony wasn't lost on Raphael. He opened his mouth to comment but Gabriella gave him a warning nudge. If she'd seen the exchange Amanda chose to ignore it and addressed her audience.

'It's imperative that we take charge of Big Ed's soul until we decide what to do with him,' Amanda didn't want another evil bastard to be let loose into the ether. 'We've no idea what their plans are for him but I suspect the opposition will be fierce. I want his father too. He's pathetic but still a trouble-maker.'

'What's the plan for the father?' asked Raphael.

'The cave.' Amanda hoped to get rid of Big Ed's father before the final showdown at Big Ed's mortal death. The teenager had been a constant irritation but Gabriella had reported an increase in his powers since returning from his last incarnation as a mosquito.

'Your sister thinks he's getting worse,' she didn't need to explain that sometimes evils appeared to have a power surge when one of their particularly bad relatives was close to accompanying them. They all remembered the disastrous results of an earlier time that this had happened and poor Zach was still down there, having suffered torture and immeasurable humiliation no doubt. They discussed various scenarios and plans for the way forward and countless examples of *what ifs*. Big Ed couldn't be banished to the cave with his father, the demons would fight to regain his soul so they would have to keep his soul moving, probably in short spells of life where he could be humiliated and have time to reflect on his past sins.

'I don't think they'll be that bothered about the father; he's merely a lackey and isn't rated. In fact,' she looked as if she'd had a brainwave. 'If you have the opportunity before I arrive let Claire deal with him, under supervision of course.'

'Brilliant idea,' Raphael smiled. 'It'll do her the world of good when she discovers just how powerful she's become and,' he clapped a tune with his hands. 'Will give her confidence and make her less frightened for the big showdown.'

'We're not in a western movie, Raphael.'

An admonishment from his mother could make him feel about five years old and the euphoria from moments before quickly slipped away.

'What if it makes her over-confident?' asked Gabriella and their discussions continued, covering all aspects of Big Ed's earthly destruction.

Much later, exhausted due to the planning and worry if anything went badly wrong, they agreed to go their separate ways and retire to their quarters to rest, before Raphael joined the others on the living plain. Their farewells were filled with melancholy as they confirmed that the next time they'd meet would be when Raphael called for his mother's and sister's assistance. None were exactly sure how long that would be in Earth time, but they knew it would be weeks rather than months.

Chapter 15

The teenager looked down at his spirit body in satisfaction. He always hated being an animal, which inevitably meant a punishment of pain. This was a good time for him, back in his comfortable earthly human body and not long before he would be joined by his son. He knew his standing would improve shortly after his son's death and hoped for an increase in power. He was almost certain that he'd go up a few grades and at long last receive the respect he deserved. Knowing he still had a little time before his son's ultimate journey, he wondered whether it was worth the risk to visit the woman his son held a torch for. He'd been amazed when he'd discovered this was one and the same woman who he'd helped some boys attack. That amazement had turned to anger when the teenager remembered the suffering he'd had to go through when her attackers had been caught. Throwing caution to the wind and knowing he was already getting stronger, he decided he had time to teach her a lesson before his son's arrival.

Some of the wedding guests were relaxing at the hotel. Val had returned from buying her tickets and sightseeing, and decided to check in with Marion before going to her room to change into her swimming costume. From the outside bar she scanned the pool area.

'Cooeee, Marion,' she called and Marion put down her Kindle and squinted in the direction of the bar. Seeing her friend, she put on her sarong and made her way toward her.

'Nice morning?' asked Marion but she could see that Val was dying to tell her something.

'Well, I did a bit of sightseeing and stuff and had a really pleasant morning...'

'And?'

'Walking back to the hotel and it was really weird, Marion. I nearly got knocked over.'

'Oh, Jesus. Are you okay?' Marion looked Val over and couldn't see any obvious marks.

'I'm fine but it felt as if someone pushed me off the kerb but there was no-one behind me.'

'That's weird. I wonder...'

Val cut her off. 'That's not the only thing. The driver who swerved to avoid me said that someone else took control of the steering wheel and he would have hit me if they hadn't'

'Have you been drinking?'

'No, seriously, Marion, it was strange. I'm lucky...What the...'

They both moved back involuntary as one of the heavy wooden roof supports dropped from the bar and hit the ground where they'd been standing. Looking at each other in confusion, Marion had felt a push and knew without it she would be under the timber. She shuddered.

'I think a guardian angel's looking out for me today,' said Val and this time Marion didn't contradict her.

'I don't know how much more of this I can take,' said Claire. 'He seems to be a lot stronger and I'm absolutely exhausted. She looked at the other two. Sandy had a hand on Ron's arm in support and was chewing her bottom lip. Ron looked as distressed as Claire had ever seen him.

'I'd help if I could, Claire. You have to be strong, you're the only who can save her.'

The teenager appeared in front of them, a look of triumph already on his face. He hadn't expected to see her and her groupies here and it was a bonus. From previous experience he knew she was strong and talented. But he also knew that his powers had increased ten-fold and there was no way she could beat him this time. He'd had much more time on this side than she and she didn't have the support of her mentors. Taking her to hell would be a masterstroke and he was sure his rewards would be plenty. He wanted a bit of fun first and Claire didn't realise what was happening until she heard both Sandy and Ron scream. They were trying their best but it was like a goldfish trying to overcome a polar bear, neither had the strength or power to fight the teenager. Claire summoned her inner resources; the evil had made a major error. Had he fought one-to-one with Claire he might have won, but she hated bullies and had stood up for kids who were being bullied once or twice while she was in school, regardless of the size of their aggressor or their gang. Claire had the same feeling now.

'I don't think so,' she said, and he was surprised at how calm she sounded as he turned to face her. Claire addressed Ron and Sandy. 'Give me your hands and form a circle around him,' still writhing in pain neither moved. 'Now! Concentrate!' the latter was a command and both moved without thinking. The teenager was encircled but not worried. Looking for the weakest link he lunged at Sandy with his full body weight and although she screamed in pain, she held on to Ron and Claire's hand, the circle unbroken. 'Remember what to think,' said Claire and though hard, they all thought of love and pleasant memories. Claire moved the circle toward the teenager wishing that Raphael and Gabriella were available to help but determined to do the job without them if necessary. She seemed to instinctively know what to do and the teenager had the first doubts about his power. He decided to call for assistance but his request bounced off the good spirits and their circle of love, and got no further. Gaining in confidence Claire told the others to close their eyes and to move nearer to the teenager. No longer frightened, they followed her order.

Raphael was watching from a discreet distance ready to assist if required. His heart swelled with love and pride for Claire. He'd expected her to form the circle, but then expected indecision as she contemplated what to do next. He knew she was a natural when he saw her instincts take over.

Knowing he'd lost he was waiting to be blown away and turned into some hideous animal, but it didn't happen that way. As the circle moved toward him he couldn't even look into their eyes and try to send evil vibes directly into their souls. A bright light seemed to envelop him and he felt an indescribable, crushing pain. He could still see and he looked in horror as his body shrunk until it was no more than a ball of bright light. The dazzling ball of light turned to one of complete and total darkness and the teenager felt himself being hurled through the atmosphere. Not sure how much later he landed with a thud and that was the last thing he remembered. It was the smell that eventually brought him back to consciousness, the totally overpowering rancid smell of ammonia. Opening his eyes it took the teenager a few seconds to adjust to the lack of light. When he eventually could see, his vision of the world was in mosaics. Something bumped into him and he started as the headless cockroach climbed over him. He realised he had antenna and checked himself over. It slowly dawned on him that he was in *the* cave that he hadn't believed existed and would spend his eternity as a cockroach. His scream echoed around the cave chambers accompanied by thousands of others, but nobody heard and nobody who counted, even cared.

All pain had disappeared and all Ron now felt, along with Claire and Sandy, was total elation. Although he knew it was mainly down to Claire, he was delighted that they'd managed to banish the teenager for all eternity. Ron felt light-headed and as if a great weight had been lifted off his shoulders.

'We've saved Val again, Claire and I just know she's going to be all right.'

Claire didn't answer. Raphael appeared and they hugged as if they hadn't seen each other for an eternity.

'Come on,' Ron said to Sandy and they disappeared back to the hotel to give the lovebirds a bit of privacy.

*****

When Val and Marion had explained what happened to the newlyweds, the youngsters were concerned for the safety of their mothers. Thankfully no further episodes had taken place but the twins still wondered what was going on. As far as Libby was concerned the accidents were a game changer and she wanted to accompany the twins to follow her mother. She was already feeling apprehensive but now felt even more nervous.

'Which is another reason why you should stay at the hotel, babe.'

'Don't *babe* me!' said Libby, hands on hips and spoiling for a fight. Tony could see that a change of tack was needed.

'I want to ensure your mother's safety, Libby and the capture of the bastard who kidnapped Mel. If you came along I'd be worried about you...' he put up his hand when she went to interrupt. 'I know you can look after yourself, but it's my job to look after you too, I'm a man and it's the way my genes are programmed. I can't help myself,' he shrugged. 'If anything was to happen to you, Libby, I'd never forgive myself.'

She conceded he had a point and he saw her visibly relax. 'Great. So the little woman stays at home and worries,' she said it with a hint of a smile and he was relieved that she'd seen sense.

Tony went to the bathroom to get ready. The twins had tried to contact Claire to no avail the previous day, so he jumped when she contacted him as he was about to shave.

'Do you have to do that?' he put a piece of toilet paper on the small cut to his chin.

'Sorry, but I thought you'd want to talk.'

'You don't half pick your moments, Claire. What was all that about yesterday?'

She gave him the gist of what had happened but left out the details of the cave. She was also tempted to tell her brother about their ancestry, but knowing he'd ask questions that she couldn't yet answer, decided to wait.

Claire left telling Tony that she'd be back when the twins needed her. He contemplated her news and was stunned by the information but glad to know that one less baddie would be involved with them today. She'd told him that they should watch their own backs as well as Val's and he was once again glad that Libby and Fiona would remain at the hotel, along with the rest of the family. Knowing how Libby picked up on his feelings Tony tried his best to remain confident and calm. When she asked him what was wrong he managed to convince her that he was nervous and would be fine when him and Jim got going.

*****

They made sure that Val didn't see them while boarding the ferry and watched as she made her way to the café on-board. Another passenger hadn't been so careful and as Jim and Tony headed toward their cabin, Jim suddenly pulled his brother along a corridor in a different direction and put a finger to his lips. Tony remained quiet as told and soon discovered the reason for his brother's diversion. Graham realised too late that he'd been discovered and didn't even attempt a lie.

'Fair cop, but how did you know.'

'Just put it this way, Dad, you'd never make a good Private Detective.' They laughed good-naturedly knowing that they couldn't exactly tell their father to go back now.

Must be their special training Graham thought as he wished he'd been more careful before concluding that they would have discovered any non-professional. That acknowledgment made him feel better about being caught. The twins reluctantly told their father who Val was due to meet and he spent the rest of the crossing trying to come to terms with the fact that he might meet the man who could have ended his daughter's life.

The journey proceeded without further drama and just after 4 pm a voice announced that they would arrive at their destination in ten minutes. The ferry docked and cars and passengers disembarked. They kept a discreet distance as Val stood at the dockside looking about her and at the map in her hand. She turned the map around and headed off and Jim chuckled. 'Typical woman, has to have it in the direction she's facing.' Graham didn't mention that he always did the same and they followed slowly, taking care not to get too close.

They hadn't been walking for long when the twins heard their sister's voice. 'She's heading for the Oasis hotel. Pretend to phone your spy HQ and act as if they've found out about the booking. That way you can hang around the area and surprise Big Ed if the cops don't beat you to it.'

'You all right, boys? You look as if you're concentrating on something?'

'Fine, Dad. I just need to make a quick phone call. I'll catch you both up.'

Graham nodded knowingly at Jim as they walked ahead. Claire's plan worked and her father was now even more convinced that his sons were some sort of special agents. When Tony caught up with them, the easiest way forward was to let his father think what he wanted.

'They're booked into the Oasis hotel and I've got directions. The, err, perp has had cosmetic surgery and we'll receive a... a signal if he appears in our line of sight.'

Jim thought Tony was overdoing it but their father was completely absorbed in the subterfuge and loving every minute of it by the look on his face.

'Let's get going then,' Tony played the part well and took the lead following Claire's directions. Graham assumed he had a miniature microphone in his ear and was taking orders from his chain of command. They'd explained the plan on the ferry and he knew his daughter's kidnapper would be caught. As well as being as excited as a five year old on Christmas Eve, Graham couldn't wait to see the man brought to justice and hoped he'd lie rotting in a foreign jail until dying of old age.

*****

Gary's week had got better and better. His test results had come back negative and the doctor confirmed that he'd been suffering from a virus. Combined with seasickness this was bound to have made him weak. Having taken the course of antibiotics he was starting to feel like his old self and had regained a little weight, though was still a lot lighter than he wanted to be. He knew it would take time to rebuild his strength and hoped that Val still found him attractive. Gary smiled to himself. He'd just concluded his business and when they'd seen the girls paraded in front of them, gave him his outrageous asking price with no questions asked. He felt no guilt or remorse for what the sick bastards would do to those girls, just relief that he'd got away with it. Daniel had been paid off and dismissed and he'd be happy to never see that scumbag again. There was only one blot on Gary's landscape and that was Captain Saul. He knew deep down that the girls hadn't just disappeared despite what the captain had told him. As soon as he felt stronger, Gary vowed to himself that he'd find Saul and teach him a lesson that he would never forget. He didn't want to think about that today though, his priority was Val and he couldn't remember when he'd last been so looking forward to seeing a woman.

*****

The bus conveying the girls had been driven out of town. The man sitting in the front row of the bus answered his phone and acknowledged the voice on the other end. He hung up after a short conversation and spoke to the driver. The bus took a few turns and stopped in a car park. The girls looked out of the window at the ambulances and cars and lots of women who were smiling at them. They were told to leave the bus and the women took their hands and gave them sandwiches and soft drinks. Tamara was suspicious and thought it was some sort of trap but accepted the refreshments. It wasn't long before she realised that they'd been rescued and she cried with relief, knowing that her nightmare had at last ended. Warm friendly arms engulfed her in a comforting hug and she took a breath, happy to be rescued from a life of sexual slavery

208

and hoping that those who kidnapped her all those months ago would get their just desserts.

*****

Walking across a low bridge on his way to the hotel where they'd arranged to meet, Gary stopped to look at the view. Sea underneath and as far as the eye could see in one direction and to the other, mountains and the landscape of the town buildings. Val would love it here he was sure. A sudden movement caught his eye and he stopped daydreaming. His sixth sense had kept him alive and free for this long and he'd always trusted his gut instinct. Something wasn't right. He looked around and saw a big man quickly turn his back and walk around a corner. Easy, he thought to himself as he carried on walking, but slowing his pace down, his eyes scanned as much of the area as they could. On the other side of the road a man leaned against a shop window, talking into a phone. Another up ahead of him looked out of place as he walked in Gary's direction. Gary kept walking but looked behind. Identical twins, he knew them! His mind quickly returned to the kidnapped girl and he remembered where he'd seen them before. Beginning to feel like a cornered rat, Gary started looking for possible escape routes. They seemed to be coming at him from all directions and he only had one choice. He ran and leaped over the metal railings, his body making a splash as it crashed into the water.

From a distance Graham looked on in disbelief as at least six men ran to the railings and looked down into the water. He couldn't believe that none of them had jumped in after him. He started running, taking off his valuables and anything he thought might weigh him down. The twins watched in amazement as their father took a jump then disappeared.

Graham was swimming as fast as he could and was making headway on his prey. Gary was a poor

209

swimmer and he caught up with him sooner than he'd expected. The man was struggling to breathe. Graham had fantasised about catching this man, letting his mind run riot with the list of punishments he'd bestow on him. There was still a look of arrogance in his eyes and it was this that spurred Graham on. He threw a misjudged punch that missed but was able to grab him by the hair. He pushed his head under the water and felt a sadistic pleasure as the evil bastard struggled underneath him. No longer able to see into the arrogant eyes, Graham's even temper began to return and he knew he didn't have it in him to kill a man in cold blood, even one who'd kidnapped his own daughter. He loosened his hold and Gary's head popped above the surface. Gasping for breath he had no interest in fighting. When he eventually stabilised he looked at his attacker trying to work out how he knew him. The man looked oddly familiar but Gary couldn't place him.

'Mel's doing well, no thanks to you,' treading water they both turned around at the sound of an engine and when Gary saw the marine police logo, knew that all further thoughts of escape were pointless.

'I hope you rot in hell, you bastard!'

Two of the crew leaned over and dragged both men onto the boat. They cuffed Gary and gave Graham a towel and a blanket.

*****

Val looked up from the magazine she was scanning. The sirens had been loud enough to wake the dead and she wondered briefly what had happened. A few of the other patrons had been outside for a look and when she asked the waiter who brought her coffee, he told her that an international criminal had been caught and would be put to justice. Val smiled to herself, wondering if Gary had been involved in the capture. She was so looking forward to seeing him and hoped he wouldn't be delayed much longer; he was already nearly twenty minutes late.

Chapter 16

The British Government were in negotiations with the Algerians to try and extradite the man who currently went by the name of Gary Jamieson, but who the police knew as Big Ed Walton. The progress was slow but in the meantime Gary was spending his days in El Harrach, the main prison in Algiers. He was crowded into a room with lots of other men, sanitary conditions were poor and the place stank. The locals received visits from some of their families once a week but not so for Gary. He felt himself weakening and the virus that hadn't completely left his body returned with gusto. But that was the least of Gary's problems. He'd heard that the Daddy was on the prowl and the rumour mill that a prisoner had died under suspicious circumstances the previous week did nothing to allay his concerns. Gary looked up as the blackest man he'd ever seen entered the room. He guessed he was about 6' 6" and his chest looked as if it would rival an average silverback. The fact that he was dressed in civilian clothes that were in pristine condition wasn't lost on Gary. There weren't many men who were bigger than Gary when he was in his prime, but this was one of them. Two smaller men followed him, his bitches Gary assumed. They spoke to the other prisoners in their own language and the prisoners got up and left the crowded room as quickly as their legs could carry them. The bitches laughed and said something to the big man and he spoke while looking all the time at Gary.

*****

It was almost time and Raphael took Claire's hand and gave it a squeeze. 'I'm going to send Ron and Sandy back, okay?' Claire nodded and said her goodbyes. Although Ron protested, he was glad to go now that he knew there was no chance of Val being hurt by Gary or Big Ed or whatever the man was calling himself these days.

'See you later,' he said and gave Claire a quick hug. He didn't want to make a big deal of the goodbye, knowing that if their efforts didn't go to plan he might never see her again. Sandy followed Ron's lead and as they left Raphael called for Gabriella and his mother.

*****

Gary shouted for the prison warders but none came. For one of the few times in his life he was scared because he knew he didn't stand a cat in hell's chance against the big fella. He recognised the look in the man's brown eyes, which mirrored that of his own before committing holy hell and he braced for the attack. His mind was working overtime trying to come up with a plan that would cause him the least grief. Maybe if he showed the big fella what an evil bastard he could be the man might recruit him to his team, and Gary would work with him until he was strong enough to mount a challenge. The bitches walked toward him and he was determined to take at least one of them out. Focusing on the smaller man on the right he tried not to give the game away. He pounced but the guy dodged his move and the other man shot around the back of Gary, and he felt something hard make contact with his shoulder. The pain from the metal rod was excruciating and he fell to his knees in agony. They made light work of tying his hands around his back and though frightened, he made eye contact with their leader and the look he gave him was one of defiance. The leader circled Gary unhurriedly and said something in his own language. As the two men pushed Gary onto his side on the stinking floor he knew that the warders wouldn't be putting in an appearance any time soon, and that they could take as much time as they wanted. He prepared himself for a good kicking but gasped when their actions showed him what was going to happen next. He

213

doubled his efforts calling for the warders until a smelly rag was shoved in his mouth and he could shout no more.

'Not long now,' said Amanda. 'This isn't going to be pretty to watch so make sure we're ready as soon as it's finished.' No one said a word as they turned back to the scene below.

'I had three children,' said the leader as he undid his trainers. 'One girl and two boys and now I have only two boys,' he nodded to the men and they removed Gary's tatty flip-flops and pulled down the bottom of his prison suit.

'An evil bastard kidnapped my girl two years ago, along with eight others and she's now dead, murdered by dirty bastards who get off by sticking their dicks in innocent children,' the man undid his jeans and slipped them off. Even though he was still wearing pants, Gary could see that his prick was stood to attention and his eyes almost bulged out of his head at the size of it. Knowing his fate he writhed and struggled but had underestimated the strength of the two smaller men who had him in a vice-like grip.

'I'm in here because all the men involved are now dead and I'm going to rid the world of dirty bastards who prey on innocent children.'

The words faded as the metal rod they used to hit Gary earlier was inserted into his anus. He screamed but no sound came out. The object was removed and he was pulled up, the men forcing him into position for their leader. Gary screamed again as the leader tore away at him and he felt his insides being ripped to shreds. The mental anguish was worse than the physical pain and tears of humiliation and shame escaped from his eyes as he felt the Daddy's disgusting moves, and listened to him telling him what a dirty bastard he was. Eventually he climaxed and withdrew. The man dressed as if nothing untoward had happened and Gary wondered if he'd ever recover from the humiliation. He needn't have worried. The man smiled at him and said something to his bitches. Gary saw the glint of steel and they untied him and each grabbed an arm.

'You will go to hell, but not just yet,' said the big man and he left the room chuckling to himself as if someone had told a very funny joke.

They managed to cut his wrists while he was still struggling and ignoring the blood, they tied his hands again but this time in front of him so that he could see his life-blood oozing from the wounds. The pain was excruciating and every time Gary felt he was about to lose consciousness they brought him back. When the blood clotted they deepened the cut and he begged and screamed and cried but no noise came out. Eventually he lost consciousness for the final time and met his death with blessed relief.

The sight of Gary's death had sickened Claire. As much as she despised the vile creature she found watching anyone's suffering hard to bear. The angels felt the same but they had had centuries to condition themselves and build their own personal protective barriers. She watched with the others as the gruesome hands pulled and prodded then started to drag his soul downwards.

'It's time,' said Amanda and Claire shook herself out of her reverie and prepared for action. Seeing the others join hands to form a circle she followed suit and they sped through the atmosphere at an exhilarating pace, followed very closely by three hosts of angels all prepared for the fight.

There were too many evils around Gary's soul so Amanda called an order to the other angels. Claire tried to pay attention to what was happening as both good and evil souls flew past her, some in an upward direction and some downward. She looked at the other three in her circle. Their eyes were shut tight and she could see the look of concentration deep on all of their faces. She didn't need to be told what to do next but still found it difficult to ignore what was going on around her and to close her own eyes. As soon as she did a veil of peace and love descended upon her and Claire immediately started thinking of love and goodness. The circle shuddered and she knew they were under attack. She felt pain and assumed correctly that the evils had targeted her as the weakest link. Claire fought a mental battle to ignore the pain and think only of lovely things. She thought she was winning and when Gabriella's voice announced *we have him* Claire relaxed her guard - a fatal error. She didn't feel any prodding hands but a sensation of travelling downwards. She heard Raphael shouting and knew instinctively to keep her eyes closed and renew her concentration one hundred fold. She shuddered to a halt and soon the direction had changed and she was on the up. Gentle hands took hold of hers and she was part of the circle once again. She sensed that something wasn't right and opened her eyes. The picture below her was her worse nightmare. Raphael was being pulled by thousands of hands. Their eyes locked and the unspoken message was for her to stay with the circle.

'Let him go, there's nothing we can do,' Gabriella's voice confirmed what they wanted from her, just in case she hadn't understood Raphael's unspoken instruction.

Claire thought she'd lost the love of her life when she'd died. She'd been lucky to find Raphael and if they thought she'd simply give him up without a fight, then they didn't know her very well at all. If he was going to hell she'd either go with him or save him, after all, he'd saved her from the horrendous fate. Her resolve wavered when she thought back to the evil probing hands. Had she dwelled on them she might have faltered. Claire put all thoughts of the evils out of her mind and concentrated on her love for Raphael. Feeling the need to make her actions known, she remembered watching a black and white TV series as a child. 'Geronimo,' she called as she flew downwards through the ether, intent on bringing back her angel.

'I don't believe it,' said Gabriella, trying to work out whether Claire was totally stupid or brave beyond belief.

Amanda summoned all her strength and launched Gary's soul to Gabriella.

'Look after him until we return.' She watched the tail end of Claire disappear after her son and smiled to herself. The girl had talent and gusto and it would take all her strength and cunning to bring them both back. 'Go home,' she said to Gabriella. 'And deal with this one. I'll take the hosts and bring them back.' Amanda recognised the look from her daughter but wasn't in the mood for an argument. 'We don't have much time and I need you there, just in case.' Gabriella wasn't happy with the role given to her but got the message loud and clear. She watched as her mother and the others followed Claire and Raphael, all spoiling for a fight, but none of them confident of the outcome.

Epilogue

Cindy closed the tall double-doors to her mansion and tried to frown. Her forehead hardly moved and she was glad the injections were doing their job but frustrated that the naughty driver was late. She flicked back her almost white blonde shoulder length hair with a perfectly manicured hand and looked at her nails wondering if the French manicure had been the right decision or if she should have gone for her trademark lemon. A bark no more than a squeak diverted her attention to the lemon handbag containing one of the world's ugliest breed of dog. To Cindy she was a cutie-pie and her squashed face was beautiful in a doggie sort of way. The dog's jacket exactly matched the colour of the bag and had its head been covered, an onlooker might not have noticed the perfectly camouflaged animal.

'Oooh, Eddie, diddums,' said Cindy. 'Are you a good girl? Is Eddie a good girl?' Her voice was almost as highly pitched as the dog's bark and she lifted it out of the bag and held it to her as if it were a baby.

'I'm a fucking, Pekingese and I'm female!' thought the dog fleetingly as he looked up at the vision in lemon whose voice grated on him like fingernails being dragged down a blackboard.

Cindy misinterpreted the look from her beloved Eddie. 'Well cheeky girl, you pee pee in my pretty handbag and that's what happens,' she now held the dog in front of her and Eddie looked down to see the lemon coloured nappy on his nether regions. It dawned on him that as well as being female, he was dressed in a lemon coat and a lemon dog nappy. Despite what had happened prior to his death, he couldn't imagine feeling more humiliated. He'd often heard people look at dogs in bows or clothes and comment that it was a good job they couldn't feel embarrassed. Well newsflash, they damn well could!

Cindy giggled, leaned forward and rubbed noses with her dog. The animal barked and its eyes looked as if they were about to pop out when it received an electric shock from its crystal studded training collar.

'Naughty girl,' said Cindy. 'Mamma's going to take you to meet Raymond and you're going to make some baby Eddies.' she gave the dog a big kiss leaving a layer of bright lipstick on its head. Big Ed knew that whatever torture he'd have to endure in future, this really was his own Hell on Earth and the sooner he departed this particular life the better.

He could stand it no more and when she loosened her grip slightly to return him to her bag he saw a chance for escape. He nipped Cindy hard enough to draw blood and shocked, she dropped him onto the driveway. Eddie ran as fast as his little legs would carry him into the path of the approaching chauffeur-driven car. The driver didn't see him and Cindy screamed as her prized possession was squashed under the front tyre. Eddie felt immense pain and intense relief as his soul left his body.

The gnarled hands started prodding instantly but these were soon accompanied by firm but gentle hands, and eventually the latter won out. Something wasn't right thought Big Ed until he opened his eyes again.

He looked down at himself dressed in a lilac coat and matching nappy on his nether regions, then he looked at the person holding the bag he was in. She looked like a dumb blonde he thought as his eyes took in the vision in lilac in front of him. Confused, he looked at himself again. 'I'm a fucking, Pekingese and I'm female!' he said as he experienced a strange feeling of deja vu.

'We're going to meet Jeremy and make baby Fifi's,' said the woman as she tickled him under his chin. A slow growl left his throat as he planned to escape from this living nightmare as soon as he was able...

*****

Gabriella sighed. The last battle had been tough and had Claire not disposed of the man's father, might have been too close for comfort. Although good had prevailed over evil, none of them yet knew whether her mother, Raphael and Claire were on their way back or had been taken by the other side. Gabriella had enjoyed the praise from God and the other members of the Committee, but couldn't even allow herself a mental pat on the back until the final outcome was known. She'd heard that her mother was no longer on the Committee but hadn't been told why – despite her bravery Gabriella knew her mother was considered a maverick and she wondered if God had been testing her, and she'd failed due to some of her questionable decisions. She also knew that her mother would be less than pleased and didn't fancy being in God's shoes on her return. She couldn't bear to think that they may not return and when God had offered her a place on the Committee Gabriella had turned it down. She knew she was mad, but had seen how it had restricted Raphael and they were similar in so many ways. She was happier fighting the never-ending evil that pervaded all of their lives, and didn't know if she'd ever be ready for a place on the Committee. If the worst happened she would need to fight to bring them back rather than have her wings clipped and sit around making decisions. Whatever the outcome, it would take both sides quite some time to recover and gain total domination in the future.

*****

220

Amanda, Raphael and Claire were preoccupied trying to save each other and avoid hell's gates. They didn't notice what was going on in a cave deep below the ground where bats and cockroaches were going about their normal daily lives. They were all totally oblivious to the large number of serpents amassing outside, and so were the Committee.

Acknowledgements

Thanks to my husband Allan for listening (or doing a good job of pretending to listen), to my fabulous editor Jill Turner and wonderful cover designer Jessica Bell. Thanks also to all my friends for their support.

Author's Note

Thank you for purchasing this book. I hope you enjoyed reading it as much as I did writing it.

If you like what you've read so far, you may be interested in my other books:

Beyond Destiny (The Afterlife Series Book 3)
Beyond Possession (The Afterlife Series Book 4)
Beyond Limits (The Afterlife Series Book 5)
Beyond Sunnyfields (The Afterlife Series Book 6) coming soon

Unlikely Soldiers Book 1 (Civvy to Squaddie)
Unlikely Soldiers Book 2 (Secrets & Lies)
Unlikely Soldiers Book 3 (Friends & Revenge)
Unlikely Soldiers Book 4 (Murder & Mayhem)

The Island Dog Squad Book 1 (Sandy's Story) - FREE AT THIS LINK
https://dl.bookfunnel.com/wdh6nl8p08

The Island Dog Squad Book 2 (Another Crazy Mission)
The Island Dog Squad Book 3 (People Problems)

Court Out (A Netball Girls' Drama)

Non-fiction:

Zak, My Boy Wonder

And for children:

Reindeer Dreams
Jason the Penguin (He's Different)
Jason the Penguin (He Learns to Swim)

Further information is on my website https://debmcewansbooksandblogs.com or you can connect with me on Facebook:
https://www.facebook.com/DebMcEwansbooksandbl ogs/?ref=bookmarks

Following a career of over thirty years in the British Army, I moved to Cyprus with my husband to become weather refugees.

I've written children's books about Jason the penguin and Barry the reindeer, and books for a more mature audience about dogs, the afterlife, soldiers and netball players, along with a non-fiction book about a very special boy named Zak.

'Court Out (A Netball Girls' Drama)' is a standalone novel. Using netball as an escape from her miserable home life, Marsha Lawson is desperate to keep the past buried and to forge a brighter future. But she's not the only one with secrets. When two players want revenge, a tsunami of emotions is released at a tournament, leaving destruction in its wake. As the wave starts spreading throughout the team, can Marsha and the others escape its deadly grasp, or will their emotional baggage pull them under, with devastating consequences for their families and team-mates?

The Afterlife series was inspired by ants. I was in the garden contemplating whether to squash an irritating ant or to let it live. I wondered whether anyone *up there* decides the same about us and thus the series was born. Book six is currently in the planning stage and I'm not yet sure when the series will end.

'The Island Dog Squad' is a series of novellas told from a dog's point of view. It was inspired by the rescue dog we adopted in 2018. The real Sandy is a sensitive soul, not quite like her fictional namesake, and the other characters are based on Sandy's real-life mates.

'Zak, My Boy Wonder', is a non-fiction book co-written with Zak's Mum, Joanne Lythgoe. I met Jo and her children when we moved to Cyprus in 2013. Jo shared her story over a drink one night and I was astounded, finding it hard to believe that a family could be treated with such cruelty, indifference and a complete lack of compassion and empathy. This sounded like a tale from Victorian times and not the twenty-first century. When I suggested she share her story, Jo said she was too busy looking after both children – especially Zak who still needed a number of surgeries – and didn't have the emotional or physical energy required to dig up the past. Almost fourteen years after Zak's birth, Jo felt ready to share this harrowing but inspirational tale of a woman and her family who refused to give up and were determined not to let the judgemental, nasty, small-minded people grind them down.

When I'm not writing I love spending time with Allan and our rescue dog Sandy. I also enjoy keeping fit and socialising, and will do anything to avoid housework.